THE DIFFICULT JOB OF KEEPING TIME

Dyan Sheldon

WALKER BOOKS

For Bobbie

This is a work of fiction. Names, characters, places and incidents are
either the product of the author's imagination or, if real, are used fictitiously.

First published 2008 by Walker Books Ltd
87 Vauxhall Walk, London SE11 5HJ

2 4 6 8 10 9 7 5 3 1

Text © 2008 Dyan Sheldon
Cover artwork © 2008 Mandy Field

The right of Dyan Sheldon to be identified as author of
this work has been asserted by her in accordance with
the Copyright, Designs and Patents Act 1988

This book has been typeset in Sabon and SoupBone

Printed and bound in Great Britain by CPI Bookmarque Ltd, Croydon, CR0 4TD

British Library Cataloguing in Publication Data:
a catalogue record for this book
is available from the British Library

ISBN 978-1-84428-110-7

www.walkerbooks.co.uk

Contents

Stories Have to Begin Somewhere, and This One Begins Here

Halfway up the hill, and set well back from the main road, three enormous concrete towers rise above the dingy streets of houses and shops, as though they were designed by a deranged, egomaniacal king to touch the heavens. (In fact, they were built by well-paid architects and city-planners to cram as many people into as small a space as possible.) The roofs of the tower blocks are decorated with satellite dishes and television aerials, the balconies with washing lines, bicycles, rusting barbecues, old paint tins and the occasional (usually dying) pot plant. Grey, grim and remorseless, the towers look so dismal and wretched that it's almost surprising that there isn't a sign over the entrance of each saying: Abandon Hope All Who Enter Here.

One of these towers is called Wat Tyler House. Like the others, Wat Tyler House gives the impression that it must always have been here, rising like a tree from the plastic bags and fast food containers that litter the ground, but, of course, it hasn't. Once there were modest rows of Victorian terraces here. The terraces themselves stood where there was once a sprawl of cottages and small farms. Which stood where there was once a Celtic settlement. Which stood where there was once a prehistoric sacred site. Which stood where there was once a dense forest filled with bears and lions and (once upon a distant time) elephants and woolly mammoths. Which stood where there was once an endless, churning sea. All that remains of any of these things – all that can be seen, at any rate – is St Barnabas, the crumbling brick church across from Wat Tyler House. St Barnabas has been here for over three hundred years, but it is unlikely to be here much longer. For, at this precise moment in time, there is a large blue and yellow van parked in the grounds. In the van, the driver dozes while he waits for the mobile phone on the seat beside him to ring. In the back of the van is a stack of signs that say that the Futures Development Corporation, Ltd, is going to build luxury flats with underground parking and a gym on this location, that the site is guarded by dogs as well as men – and that trespassers will be prosecuted (if not actually torn limb from limb).

Two hundred families – or parts of families – live in Wat Tyler House, stacked one on top of the other like tins of beans on a supermarket shelf (which makes it quite a success at cramming as many people into as small a space as possible – if at nothing else). Many of these people couldn't tell you who lived across the hall, or even next door, never mind a few floors above or below them. And most of these people hate Wat Tyler House, its gloomy, anonymous, concrete corridors and its grudging, anonymous, joyless flats, with a passion they have for nothing else. Even the fact that the tower block was named after the legendry Wat Tyler, leader of the Peasants' Revolt of 1381, doesn't make the residents feel any better about it, partly because most of them have no idea who Wat Tyler was. Often, if you look, you can see someone standing on a balcony or at a window, staring into the sky as though waiting to be rescued. But they never are.

Everyone calls it The Wat.

Amongst the hundreds of people living in The Wat are Trish O'Leary and her mother, and Kiki Monjate and his parents and brothers and sisters. And amongst the hundreds of people living within the shadow of The Wat – at least for the moment – is Betty Friedman.

Our story belongs to them, but at this point

Kiki Monjate, Trish O'Leary and Betty Friedman have yet to meet. They are, however, about to come together through a series of events that may seem like mere coincidence (if you are Trish), or bad luck (if you are Kiki), or simply what had to be (if you happen to be Betty Friedman).

I'll leave it to you to decide which of these things – if any – it actually is.

Everyone Is Afraid of Something – Even Betty Friedman

All of us are different. We look different, think differently, and act differently. Not everybody likes chocolate cake, or pop music, or even football. Not everyone likes to climb enormous mountains, or read books, or tend a garden. But if there is one single thing that unites the people on this planet, then that one thing is fear. Everybody is afraid of something – from real things, like thunder storms and air travel, to not-so-real things, like headless horsemen and vampires.

Trish O'Leary and Kiki Monjate are not exceptions to this rule.

Trish is a practical, down-to-earth sort of girl who doesn't possess what one might call an overactive imagination. If the sky turns the colour of squashed blackberries and lightening cracks it as if it's an egg, Trish knows that it isn't the end of the world, but the weather. If she hears a few bumps in the night she knows that it isn't ghosts, but her mother walking into a wall. Because of her nature, the only thing Trish is really afraid of is the ex-Mrs O'Leary. Trish's mother does have her good days, but on her bad days (which are much more frequent) she is a difficult and unhappy woman. Trish's mother is unhappy – and, therefore, difficult – because her life has not turned out the way she thinks it should have turned out. This fills her with resentment and rage.

Trish's mother directs this resentment and rage at everyone but herself (as people often do). Sometimes the ex-Mrs O'Leary blames the world in general, sometimes she blames Trish's long-gone father, or Trish, or anyone who happens to rub her up the wrong way. But it is when the ex-Mrs O'Leary is filled with alcohol – as well as rage and resentment – that she becomes especially difficult. Then she doesn't just shout and scream, she throws things, she breaks things and she hits things (and walks into walls) with all the force of her enormous despair. After eleven years of living with her mother, Trish is skilled at getting out of the way when the bric-a-brac and fists start to fly. She has learned to do without friends (she never brings anyone home because she never knows what mood her mother will be in) and has learned to fend for herself. Trish even bought and installed a lock for her bedroom door so that she is safe from the worst of her mother's fury and can sleep without the worry that she might be woken in the night by being pulled out of bed by her hair (which has happened on more than one occasion, though her mother has always apologized later). Nonetheless, living with the ex-Mrs O'Leary is a lot like living in a war zone, which is not something most of us would choose to do – and which is certainly not something that Trish would have chosen, had anyone asked her opinion before she was born.

Although always a cautious and superstitious child, until he came to Great Britain six years ago Kiki was only afraid of bad luck and bad spirits. Now he is afraid of just about everything, from the roads he walks to the air he breathes. He is even afraid of the resident ghosts, though he knows that they mean him no harm. Kiki has always seen ghosts. When he lived with his grandmother the ghosts he saw were the ghosts of his ancestors. Now they are the ghosts of other people's ancestors – women carrying firewood and water, children running through the car park and men wearing antlers, running through the traffic on the main road. Amongst the many apparitions he sees, the ones that disturb him the most are a weeping girl with hair like a sunset, kneeling by a tall stone in a corner of the churchyard, and a small procession carrying a bier containing the tiny corpse of a child covered in a white shroud straight through the side of the church.

But of all the things Kiki fears, the thing he fears the most is The Wat Boys. Unlike the ghosts, The Wat Boys *do* mean Kiki harm. There are only four of them – Brendan, Paul, Chris and Aidan – but they couldn't be more terrifying if there were thirty. The Wat Boys have quite a bit of fear themselves. To hide this they like to instil as much fear in others as they can. The Wat Boys – who, in reality, have very little that they can call their own – like to believe that The Wat belongs to them. They are older than Kiki, which is one of the few good things about them, since it means that they don't go to Kiki's school. Indeed, as they're always hanging about somewhere nearby, looking for trouble, it seems unlikely that they go to anyone's school. It is The Wat Boys who cover the walls of the tower blocks – and just about any other wall they come across – with indelible black ink. It is The Wat Boys who mug old ladies for their handbags and small children for their dinner money. It is The Wat Boys who smash windscreens and rip open bin liners. It is The Wat Boys who torment Kiki without mercy, or any sign of ever stopping.

They chase him on their bikes and throw sticks and stones at him. They threaten, amongst other things, to hang him over the railway bridge. They call him names and make fun of his clothes – from his corduroy trousers to his blue wool jacket which, apparently, is the only jacket in the city that still fastens with buttons. Indeed, the only thing that didn't draw their ridicule was the pair of trainers that Kiki's mother got for him in the charity shop, which were just like the ones all the other boys wore. The Wat Boys tore them off his feet and threw them on the roof of the bus shelter, where they still lie. If you were to ask The Wat Boys why they do these things, they wouldn't say because they are bored and angry and have nothing to look forward to but a future of debt and mindless labour (or, possibly, prison) – which would be true. Nor would they say it's because they can – which would also be true. They would say it's because Kiki isn't British and should go back to where he came from. This is an option Kiki would be happy to take up – if only he could.

Betty Friedman is afraid of very little. She certainly isn't afraid of the things that most women over ninety are afraid of (death, breaking a hip, being robbed). The only thing she really fears is that people will forget their past, that Time's memories will be lost to a world that exists only in the here and now. And it is because of all he has done to make that fear a reality that Betty Friedman loathes – nearly to the point of fear – someone she has known more or less forever but whom she hasn't seen in nearly two hundred years, and whose name, at the moment, she doesn't know.

But it truly is an ill wind that blows no one any good, and as ill as the ex-Mrs O'Leary after a bottle of wine, The Wat Boys on their bikes and Betty Friedman's age-old adversary can be, it is because of them that there is a story to tell.

Betty Friedman Attends a Meeting – and Runs into Someone She Used to Know

Betty Friedman was on her way to the airport when, as luck (or, possibly, coincidence) would have it, she found herself stuck in traffic in a particularly unattractive part of London. Dingy shops lined the dreary road, and even dingier concrete towers loomed over them, like vultures watching something die. Betty Friedman asked the driver where they were. "We're lost," he dolefully informed her. "I thought I took a shortcut, but we're lost." Betty Friedman gazed at the road and at the buildings she had never seen before. Betty Friedman wasn't so certain. She had a feeling. A feeling that this was a place she used to know very well. Which, indeed, it was. Betty Friedman's feelings are always to be trusted. In the extremely distant past this place had been her home. And long after Fate had taken her to other lives and other homes, she used to visit every century on a private pilgrimage of loss and love. But she hadn't visited for quite a long time. Indeed, she hadn't even thought of visiting, had forgotten it completely, as though the memory had been shut behind a door. As she hugged the sleeping cat on her lap closer and stared through the cab window, however, the door began to open and Betty Friedman could see what was so long gone. She saw fields and streams and woods and tracks. She saw many of the ghosts that Kiki Monjate sees, but, of course, to her they weren't ghosts, they were simply memories. In one of these memories she saw a tall, newly carved stone set in the sacred ground. The carvings on the stone were Ogham inscriptions and marked the grave of a great king. A very young woman with hair the colour of copper was kneeling beside the stone, a bracelet made of plaited hair around her wrist, her eyes filled with tears. It was then Betty Friedman knew that it was neither coincidence nor luck that had brought her here; she was where she was meant to be. When she opened her eyes again, Betty Friedman hastily paid the driver and left the car along with her cat.

Now, as she shuts the door of the outer office of Edward I. Chumbley, Minister for Housing, behind her, Betty Friedman is not in a mood to be trifled with.

The Minister's secretary looks up. An old lady in a homemade-looking skirt and bulky hand-knit jumper, a bulging carpetbag clasped in one hand and a sleeping cat cradled in her arm, is striding towards her. To the secretary's credit, although the old lady is most definitely not the sort of person she expected to see, she manages a polite smile. "May I help you?"

"I have an appointment," says Betty Friedman. And then, because this statement doesn't change the fixed smile on the secretary's face, adds, "With Mr Chumbley. I'm afraid I'm a trifle late." The miracle, of course, is that she's here at all.

The secretary makes a mental note to have a word with Security, then slowly shakes her head. "I am sorry. I don't know how you got in here—"

"I told you." Betty Friedman taps the plastic Visitor's card pinned to her jumper. "I have an appointment. I'm on the list."

The secretary's smile doesn't shift as she sighs. "I'm afraid that's impossible. The Minister is in a very important meeting. There are no appointments this afternoon."

"Three o'clock. I spoke to you myself." Betty Friedman leans over the desk, her eyes on the secretary's. "Don't you remember? Elizabeth Martha Friedman. Three o'clock."

A second ago, Mr Chumbley's secretary definitely had no such memory, but now, staring into Betty Friedman's alarmingly clear blue-green eyes, she does. She can even hear herself saying, "three o'clock, Miss Friedman, yes, that will be fine..." Flustered, she looks down at the open diary on her desk. There are three names neatly written next to the one o'clock slot, but the rest of the afternoon has a red line drawn through it, just as it should.

"Well, I'm afraid you're not here."

Betty Friedman leans a little closer. "You mean you forgot to write it down?"

The secretary looks back to Betty Friedman, and hears herself stammer, "Well, I am sorry— I don't see how— Mr Chumbley—"

"Memory loss," Betty Friedman solemnly informs her. "I'm afraid it's all too common in people your age these days. Because of the aluminium tins and pollutants, you know."

Reeling slightly with confusion the secretary says, "Well, I am sorry if there's been some sort of mistake, but I'm afraid that you'll have to make another appointment. As I told you, the Minister is in a very important meeting."

"Which is precisely why I'm here, isn't it?" says Betty Friedman very firmly. And, without seeming to move, arrives at the door with the brass plaque that reads: Edward I. Chumbley.

The secretary jumps up. "You can't go in there!"

But Betty Friedman has already opened the door and stepped through.

The purpose of the important meeting that is taking place in the office of the Minister for Housing this afternoon is to finalize the sale of the church of St Barnabas and the land on which it stands. It is not a large meeting. There are only four people in attendance: Mr Edward I. Chumbley, who has organized this sale; Councillors Wingate and Stronge, who, as representatives of their borough, are agreeing to this sale; and Sir Alistair Deuce, Chief Executive Officer of the Futures Development Corporation, Ltd, the company making the purchase.

The councillors have spoken at some length of regeneration, which is a favourite word of theirs at the moment. They have listed all the benefits that replacing the old church with modern flats will bring to the community. The words "new homes", "new businesses", "new jobs", "new attitudes" and "new energy" have been mentioned at least half a dozen times. The words "new taxes" have not.

Mr Chumbley has spoken of "the need for forward-looking planning, moral and intellectual courage and immutable progress". *Look Forward,*

Not Backward and *We Must Move On* are two of his party's most popular slogans.

Sir Alistair has spoken movingly of the "paramount importance of the partnership between the government and the private sector in improving the lives and prospects of the nation as a whole".

Each of these gentlemen has said these and similar things quite often before – usually in front of an audience – and it is extremely unlikely that anything short of the earth's collision with an asteroid will stop them from saying them again.

Indeed, to listen to these gentlemen, one would think that the demolition of St Barnabas was guaranteed to bring not only prosperity and modernity to the area, but a spiritual rebirth as well. Redemption for all the poor souls who watch the world from their cluttered balconies or on their paid-by-instalments television screens. Not much could be farther from the truth. There will be new homes, new business and new jobs, but they won't be for the people in the tower blocks. On the contrary, since the gentlemen's long-term plans include the destruction of the towers, the futures of their residents will be, if anything, even worse than they were before.

For it is a sad fact of human nature that most people act not out of goodness or a sense of right, but out of self-interest. The four men in their suits and ties who sit around the Minister's conference table, their watches, rings and (in the case of Sir Alistair) cufflinks shining like stars, are not exceptions. Chumbley, Stronge and Wingate all frequently refer to themselves as "public servants" (especially during election campaigns and media interviews), but the only public they ever serve are themselves and their friends. Sir Alistair, of course, has never – not even accidentally – served anyone but himself, or even pretended to, and he is not about to break that habit now. For all his eloquence (and sincerity) about burying the past and embracing the future, it is not the nation's good for which he strives, but control. Indeed, the men at the table are all excellent examples of the old saying that power corrupts. And proof that it doesn't have to be absolute power to corrupt absolutely. Even a little will do the job.

Up until now, this meeting, seen by all as a mere formality, has been friendly and agreeable, with a fine lunch eaten, good coffee drunk, quality cigars smoked and compliments exchanged between the four participants like kisses between sweethearts.

"Well, gentlemen, I think that it's time to sign the papers," Mr Chumbley says, his eyes on Mr Wingate and Mr Stronge. "It goes without saying that this is a momentous occasion for all of us. A day that will be remembered for a long time to come."

23

The gentlemen all nod their agreement. They certainly intend to remember it.

Mr Chumbley has just picked up the gold pen he always uses on such occasions when the door to the office suddenly flies open.

Sir Alistair, who sits facing the window, doesn't turn round, but the councillors both look over in surprise.

Mr Chumbley rises to his feet. "Just what is the meaning of this?" Mr Chumbley directs the question not to the elderly woman carrying the ratty old bag and the sleeping cat, but to his secretary, flapping behind her. "Didn't I tell you that we weren't to be disturbed?"

"I'm so sorry, Mr Chumbley. I did tell her you were in an important meeting."

"And as I've already said, that's precisely why I'm here." Betty Friedman comes to a stop between the Minister for Housing and Councillor Stronge. The sleeping cat in her arms starts to purr. Betty Friedman's eyes move from the Minister to the papers on the table. "And I see that although I am late, I am not *too* late. You haven't signed anything yet."

Mr Chumbley doesn't pause to wonder how the old woman could possibly know about this meeting – or that the papers have yet to be signed. Indeed, the only words he seems to hear are "too" and "late", and these he dutifully repeats. "Too late?" Mr Chumbley splutters. "Too late for what?"

Betty Friedman gazes at him as though this isn't a question he should have to ask. "Why, too late to raise my objections to the proposed sale of St Barnabas to the Futures Development Corporation, Ltd, of course."

"Objections?" says Councillor Stronge. "But there are no objections."

"That's right," agrees Councillor Wingate. "No objections at all."

"And there aren't going to be any now," cuts in Mr Chumbley. "It is most decidedly too late – the closing date for objections was over a week ago."

"Fiddlesticks!" Although she doesn't use it very often, especially not when addressing men in good suits, Betty Friedman has quite a sweet smile. "You all know, as well as I do, that this is a deal that was done in the dark. The reason there haven't been any objections to your project is because no one who might object was ever asked for their opinion – or even told of what you're planning."

Councillors Wingate and Stronge both turn accusingly to the Minister of Housing, as though this lapse has nothing to do with them. "Chumbley?"

Mr Chumbley straightens his shoulders and holds his head high. "I'm afraid, Madam," he says with all the authority of his office (and no trace of sorrow), "that I am going to have to ask you to leave."

"Poppycock!" snaps Betty Friedman. "I have every right to state my opinions, and if you refuse to let me state them here I shall be forced to state them elsewhere." Her smile is now so sweet that Mr Chumbley can feel it sticking to his face. "Perhaps to the press…"

At the mention of the press, Councillor Wingate and Councillor Stronge turn pale, as if the blood has been suddenly drained from their bodies, but it isn't at them that Mr Chumbley looks. Sir Alistair gives him the slightest of nods.

"Very well, if you are going to be difficult, Mrs—"

"Friedman." She extends the hand not occupied by the cat. "Elizabeth Martha Friedman."

"Mrs Friedman." Mr Chumbley takes Betty Friedman's hand with all the enthusiasm of a man taking the paw of a brown bear. Her grip is so firm that it makes him wince.

"And it's Miss."

"Miss Friedman." Mr Chumbley retrieves his fingers, flexing them to make certain none are broken. "Now, as I was saying, although it is highly irregular at this late date, I will allow you to voice your objections. That is your right, of course, but I sincerely doubt that there's anything you can tell us about the history of St Barnabas that we haven't already taken into consideration. We have the only documentation that exists for the site; the original deeds that show the church is almost two hundred years old." He gives the councillors a conspiratorial smile. "Which I'm certain we all agree hardly makes it special."

"I don't know what deeds you have, Mr Chumbley, but St Barnabas is three hundred and thirty-seven years old, actually," Betty Friedman corrects him. "And, of course, it is on the site of several much older structures, including a Roman outpost and a medieval chapel."

Councillors Stronge and Wingate exchange a look of alarm. This is news to them.

Mr Chumbley, however, is an experienced politician, skilled at ignoring inconvenient facts or questions.

"I know nothing of that. What I *do* know is that the church is in such a state of dereliction that the costs of repairing it are completely prohibitive," he purrs. "Especially since, despite what you believe to be its age, St Barnabas is of little real historical interest."

"Which is another thing you're wrong about."

Betty Friedman's bag thuds onto the tabletop. "As it happens, St Barnabas itself is of *great* historical interest. Not only was it the parish church of a great many famous writers and artists over the centuries, but its architecture is quite unique."

Councillors Stronge and Wingate, who knew nothing of any of this either, turn their look of alarm on the Minister for Housing.

Mr Chumbley smiles the smile of a man placating a lunatic. "I think you'll agree, Mrs— Miss Friedman, that the future of the community is more important than maintaining some old ruin just because someone who wrote a few poems once prayed there."

Betty Friedman meets his eyes. "And what about the graves?"

"Pardon?"

"The graves," repeats Betty Friedman. "What do you plan to do with the graves?"

"Oh, I see," Mr Chumbley chuckles condescendingly, though, in fact, he doesn't see at all. "You mean the handful of headstones round the side of the church. Well, naturally, they'll be moved to—"

"Not those graves. The twelfth century cemetery underneath them." There is something in the way Betty Friedman says this that suggests that she knows the name of every occupant in this cemetery, which, in fact, she does. "And the Roman and Celtic burial grounds beneath that."

"Ah…" Mr Chumbley doesn't look over to see the expressions on the faces of Councillors Wingate and Stronge, which is probably a good thing. Both of them suspect that they are watching not just the large sum of money they are making on this deal but also their political careers vanish before their eyes, and, as a result, don't look very well. Instead, he smoothly changes the direction of his argument. "So you've heard those ridiculous stories." His smile is as slick as oil. "But I'm afraid that's all they are, Miss Friedman. Stories. Rumours and myths. We've all heard the stories – there was a church of some sort on the site before St Barnabas, and that it was built on a sacred pagan site that contains the magical stone of some king—"

"He was a great king," interrupts Betty Friedman. "A very special and remarkable man. And it is not a magical stone, Mr Chumbley, it is a stone inscribed in the ancient Celtic alphabet of Ogham, which marks his grave. Which would make it, I believe, the only example ever found in England." She smiles back at the Minister for Housing. "Though I daresay you are far more interested in the things that were buried with him." Although they've only just met, it is clear from her tone that Betty Friedman has decided that the "I" in Mr Chumbley's name must stand for Idiot.

Mr Chumbley, who is extremely interested in the things that were buried with the king, pretends that he isn't. "Whatever you may think is there, is unimportant." Mr Chumbley has now officially stopped smiling. "The point, my dear Miss Friedman, is that none of those stories are true. There was no 'original' church, there is no cemetery, there are no Roman graves and no burial ground. And there most definitely is no sacred site or magic stone or anything of that sort."

"Balderdash," says Betty Friedman. "All of those stories are true. Those and more. That site is sacred several times over. It beats like a heart through all of time."

Mr Chumbley rolls his eyes at his associates and clears his throat. "I hate to disappointment you, Miss Friedman, but I'm afraid that the plans of the Futures Development Corporation, Ltd, fulfil all our criteria for purchasing what the government considers a relatively worthless property, beating heart through time or not."

"And what about everything else that lies *under* the church and its grounds?" Betty Friedman enquires. "What are your plans for that?"

Councillors Wingate and Stronge, who not long

ago believed that the only things under St Barnabas were clay and possibly an underground stream, exchange another look.

"Are we talking about the graves again?" asks Mr Chumbley.

"Not just the graves," Betty Friedman explains. "There have been human settlements on and around that property for nearly a million years. Many of the artefacts that are buried beneath St Barnabas are priceless. Even without the Ogham stone, there is so much of great rarity and cultural importance there that there will be no trouble having St Barnabas designated an English Heritage Site. But the stone eclipses everything else! The stone without doubt makes it a World Heritage Site. It's as important as Stonehenge or Hadrian's Wall – perhaps even more." She turns to the councillors. "I'm sure you gentlemen appreciate what that could mean to the community." The councillors assume she means money. Their eyes dart to Mr Chumbley. "And what it could be worth – in the wrong hands."

Mr Chumbley's hands, of course, are two of the wrong hands she means. And Mr Chumbley knows it. For the Minister of Housing is well aware of the artefacts buried under the church. He has been told by none other than Sir Alistair Deuce that they include Medieval chalices and manuscripts, Roman vessels and jewellery, and the sword and helmet of the Celtic King – things that are worth a fortune beyond the wildest dreams of even someone as avaricious as Mr Chumbley (who, of course, is only interested in stones if they are diamonds).

Like a murderer returning to the scene of the crime, the smile returns to Mr Chumbley's face. "And where is your proof, Miss Friedman, if I might ask? You can't simply barge in here spouting outrageous stories, and expect us to believe you. Without any proof—"

"I have proof." Without disturbing the sleeping cat, she opens her handbag and begins rummaging through it. "I have complete documentation. Including Roman records and accounts, and a very detailed history of the site that was written by one of the priests who lived there in the fourteenth century."

Mr Chumbley allows himself another eye-roll in the direction of the other men and another condescending chuckle. He nods to the bag. "In *there*?"

"Of course not. Do you think I would take things of such antiquity on the bus?" Betty Friedman removes a red, black and yellow bandanna from her bag and hands it the Minister for Housing. "I was looking for this. You seem to be perspiring rather profusely."

Mr Chumbley, who *is* perspiring rather profusely, drops the handkerchief onto the table.
"Thank you, but I'm perfectly fine." Mr
Chumbley is beginning to lose both his nerve and
his cool. "If you don't have the proof with you,
then where, precisely, do you have it?"

"Somewhere safe," says Betty Friedman.
"Somewhere very safe."

This is so much the sort of evasive answer that
Mr Chumbley himself is used to giving that he
assumes Betty Friedman must be lying, which,
unfortunately, she is. "With all due respect, Miss
Friedman, I can't help feeling that you are wasting
our time."

"I never waste time." This statement, however,
is completely true. Betty Friedman has never
wasted so much as one second. "It will take me a
day or two to get them, but—"

"And *I* don't waste time, either," says the
Minister for Housing. "Time, after all, is money."

"Rubbish," Betty Friedman closes her handbag
with a sharp click. "All the money in the world
couldn't buy you an extra second of time." Her
eyes darken. "You might do well to remember the
words of the sage, Mr Chumbley: '*If a man's
wealth is only counted in gold he will never know
heaven.*'"

Being driven everywhere in a silver Jaguar is

about the only heaven Mr Chumbley cares to know. He sighs impatiently. "My point, Miss Friedman, is that the demolition is scheduled to begin on Monday, so I'm afraid that if you can't deliver your *proof* by then..."

Councillors Wingate and Stronge have listened to this exchange in silence and growing dismay. The significance of Betty Friedman's claims has not been lost on them. If what she says is true, or even partially true, then the sooner they extricate themselves from the project, the better. They exchange another look, and both begin to gather up their things.

"I'm afraid you'll have to postpone the demolition, Mr Chumbley." Councillor Wingate pushes back his chair in the rough and angry way he'd very much like to push the Minister for Housing at this moment. "We can't possibly go ahead whilst there's any doubt about the true nature of the site."

"But you've seen the deed—" argues Mr Chumbley. "You accepted our terms. You agre—"

"There's a council meeting on Tuesday afternoon in the Town Hall." Councillor Stronge is already on his feet. "That gives Miss Friedman four days to produce this proof of hers. And if she does..." He gives Mr Chumbley a look in which disappointment and disgust are evenly matched.

"Well, then, not only is the deal off, but I should think there will be some questions asked as well."

Although the councillor wasn't actually speaking to her, it is Betty Friedman who answers. "Not to worry," she says. "I'll be there on Tuesday with the documents in hand."

"Till Tuesday, then," says Councillor Wingate.

Councillor Stronge nods. "Till Tuesday."

And they are gone with such haste that Mr Chumbley is still staring at the place where they were as the door to his office shuts behind them.

It is only then that Betty Friedman finally turns around to face the other gentleman in the room.

The other gentleman in the room, Sir Alistair Deuce, has been observing the proceedings in silence. Sir Alistair, like Betty Friedman, is not what he seems to be. And so, although the faces of his colleagues have all shown surprise, anger, fear and disappointment since the old woman barged in, Sir Alistair's expression has been difficult to read. It is only now, as Betty Friedman turns around, that the expression on his face becomes clear. It is amusement.

"Well, I'll be damned," says Sir Alistair (who probably will be), "if it isn't my oldest friend." He looks her up and down. "I see you're still making your own clothes, Aziza."

Betty Friedman, who recognized him as soon as she opened the door, of course, shows no surprise at this greeting. "It's Elizabeth now," she informs him. "And it's been quite a while since you and I were friends." Betty Friedman has the same smile she has always had – as if she knows a secret no one else will ever learn – and he still finds it irritating. "But it's nice to know that you're pleased to see me." She doesn't look at all pleased to see him. "I'm flattered that you still recognize me."

Sir Alistair raises his eyebrows in mock surprise. "And how could I not know you? That's preposterous. I knew who you were the second you walked through the door." He nods to the animal purring in the crook of her arm. "Even before I realized you had your accursed catawampus with you." He leans back in his chair as though settling himself for a pleasant chat. "But it has been a long while, hasn't it?"

It has been, in fact, nearly two hundred years.

"Could it ever be long enough?" Betty Friedman wonders aloud.

"Oh, come, come…" Sir Alistair makes a face that suggests he has feelings to be hurt. "Though I must confess, I rather feared that you were avoiding me."

"Did you?" Betty Friedman knows just who has been avoiding whom for these two hundred years.

"Oh, my dear girl…" He shakes his head regretfully. "I shouldn't want you ever to think a thing like that. You know how time flies when one's busy. And the past couple of centuries have been even busier than most." His smile makes up in unpleasantness what it lacks in charm. "For you, as well, I wager. In fact, I believe I heard that you'd gone west on one of your futile quests to save some bit of old rubbish or other."

"And you, no doubt, went east on one of your quests to destroy even more…"

Sir Alistair's laugh sounds like something trying to get out of a cage. "You haven't changed a bit, have you? Not even after all these years."

Her gaze moves from the gold rings on his fingers to his eyes, as blue and cold as glaciers. "And nor have you, I see. You're precisely as I remember you best." She absentmindedly strokes the cat, which opens its eyes to slits. "More's the pity."

Sir Alistair puts the tips of his fingers together, a gesture that in another man might suggest he was going to pray. "Tut, tut, tut. I know how grievously attached to the past you've always been, but surely you should be over all that by now. It's time you learned to forgive and forget."

Betty Friedman's voice snaps like a breaking twig. "You betrayed everything – and everyone – you were sworn to protect. Only a fool would forgive or forget a thing like that."

"And you, of course, are not a fool." If his smile were a sound it would be the one made by metal being dragged across metal. "Even if you do choose to squander your time and talents on fools' errands."

"I don't consider saving St Barnabas a fool's errand."

"Oh, really, my dear…" Sir Alistair's cufflinks, rings and watch all glint as he waves his hands dismissively. "Look at you, you obviously only just stumbled into this or you would have raised a ruckus months ago. All this trouble and bother and changing your plans, to save a few of Time's trite trinkets—" By which he means the artefacts so coveted by Mr Chumbley. "Do you really think it's worth it?"

"There is more at stake here than trinkets, and you know it." A few metres of carpet separates their bodies, but it is a universe that separates their souls. It is across that universe that their eyes look into one another's as they have on several dark occasions over the millennia. "When you lose the reminders, you lose the stories," says Betty Friedman, breaking the echoing silence.

"The sooner the better, if you ask me," answers Sir Alistair Deuce.

Stunned by the way his genial, mere-formality

meeting has changed, Mr Chumbley has been in something of a trance since the councillors marched out the door. He has heard nothing of what has been going on around him, his mind occupied with thoughts of financial ruin, political suicide and possible imprisonment. A few of Sir Alistair and Betty Friedman's words must have made it to his brain, however, for now he looks up, blinking. "Pardon me," says Mr Chumbley, "but have I missed something here?" He turns his puzzled frown to Sir Alistair. "Do you two know each other?"

Sir Alistair smiles his elsewhere smile. "Indeed we do."

"He's like a bad ha'penny," says Betty Friedman. "He always turns up again – eventually."

"Oh, my dear, that is unkind." Sir Alistair frowns as though she's hurt his feelings again. "Especially as I could very well say the same thing about you. Every time I think you're off my trail for good, there you are." He waggles a finger at the mass of grey fur draped across her arm. "You and that blasted creature."

"We are each consigned to our particular fates," says Betty Friedman as she moves to the door. "And, sadly, you seem to be stuck in mine." She puts her hand on the knob and turns with another smile. "Well, I'll see you gentlemen on Tuesday." The smile rests on Sir Alistair, and deepens. "I can hardly wait."

As soon as Betty Friedman is gone Mr Chumbley turns on his associate. "That old cow's going to ruin everything," he fumes. "How could she possibly know what's under the bloody church? Perhaps we should rethink this whole project. It isn't—"

"Surely you're not changing your mind?" Sir Alistair's eyes darken. "Not now, when we're so close to success."

"I don't know… I don't know… My career… My reputation…" Mr Chumbley shakes his head and waves his hands and groans.

"Oh, come now." The smile of the devil buying a soul was never sweeter than Sir Alistair's is now. "You're not going to let that old crone make you pass up a fortune, are you?"

It is clear from the pained expression on his face that Mr Chumbley would rather not. "But she's going to ruin everything. We've got to do something. You've got to do something."

Reassured that Mr Chumbley isn't dissolving their partnership just yet, Sir Alistair stretches in his chair as though he has only just woken from a pleasant nap. "Calm down, Edward. Do calm down. You'll give yourself a stroke." But his equanimity belies the fact that though he is amused at the turn of events, he is also annoyed. A lack of thoroughness is one of Sir Alistair's flaws. Because he counts on most people's tendency to obliterate the past, he often underestimates the ferocity with which others cling to it. He should have considered the possibility that older (and more accurate) documents existed. And that they might turn up to wreck everything. Not that he is going to admit any of this to the nervous Minister for Housing. "My money says that the old bag's bluffing. For God's sake, man, she's not a billionaire collector of antiquities. She travels by bus! She can't have the documents she claims. Assuming that they ever did exist, it's more than likely they were destroyed in the war – if not well before."

But Mr Chumbley, whose blood pressure is too high even at the best of times (which this isn't), doesn't calm down. "You can't be certain of that. What if she does have them? Or knows where they are? She seems to know everything else. About the treasure ... about our plans—"

Sir Alistair dismisses his friend's worries with a flap of one beautifully manicured hand. "You really will have a stroke if you don't get a grip on yourself. Trust me. Whether she has the documents or not, Miss Friedman is no threat to us."

41

His smile suddenly makes Mr Chumbley think of the ocean on an extremely dark night. "Not now that I know where she is."

Another of Sir Alistair's flaws is arrogance.

Trish Takes a Walk

Today is the start of the half-term break, which means that Trish has come home in a wary frame of mind. The ex-Mrs O'Leary doesn't like half-term breaks. Half-term breaks, in her opinion, are yet another example of how the world is set against her. What is she meant to do with Trish at home for an entire week? Under her feet. Making messes. Getting in her way. What the ex-Mrs O'Leary usually does during this time, of course, is absolutely nothing. No trips to the shops or the cinema; no walks along the canal or through the park; no visits to a museum or the zoo. "I wasn't put on this earth to entertain *you*," the ex-Mrs O'Leary always says. Since the reason the ex-Mrs O'Leary was put on this earth seems to be to complain, Trish tries to keep out of her way during school breaks. Since she has no friends to visit, this means that Trish spends her days in front of the telly. But no matter how still she is, or how low she has the sound, or how good she is about remembering not to leave empty plates, glasses or crisp wrappers on the coffee table, eventually something will set her mother off. "Do you have to breathe like that?" her mother once asked her. Trish said, "Yes," and went to her room. But, instead of snapping and snarling and demanding how she's meant to get anything done with Trish moping round the house, today her mother is in a good mood when Trish walks into the flat.

"Tell you what," she says to Trish. "Why don't we go down to the shops and get something special for tea. Pizza ... burgers ... anything you like."

Trish doesn't immediately believe that she and her mother are going to have one of their good nights together – nights when they watch the telly and talk and laugh – but she wants to.

"That'd be brilliant," says Trish, hope held between her crossed fingers like a thread.

Things start going wrong even before they leave the flat. Her mother can't find her keys. After Trish finds the keys for her, she can't find her purse. Then she can't get the door to lock. The lift stinks of pee and the light is out. They get stuck on the ninth floor for nearly two minutes. By the time they finally reach the ground, Trish's mother's good mood is only a fleeting memory.

They leave The Wat in the sort of dead silence that often precedes a terrific storm. And so it does now.

The ex-Mrs O'Leary trips over that dodgy bit of pavement outside the block, and then stops abruptly and starts to scream.

"Look at you!" she shrieks, her colour high and her voice even higher. "You look like you live on the street! You look like some flamin' refugee!"

"I'm just wearing my usual clothes," Trish answers flatly.

This statement, however, does nothing to calm her mother down.

"Is that what you want?" she demands – not just of Trish but of the entire neighbourhood. "To shame me in front of everyone?"

As if you need any help with that... thinks Trish, but she says nothing. Experience has taught her that the best response to her mother's public outbursts is to ignore them. There is no point in arguing or trying to reason with her – arguing and reasoning only make things worse – so she waits for the outburst to pass, which it often does.

Though not this time.

Off like a greyhound at the sound of the starter's pistol, Trish's mother keeps screaming, picking up speed and grievances as she goes. Trish is an ingrate; Trish is lazy; Trish has a bad attitude; Trish never thinks about anyone but herself.

"You're just like your father," rants the ex-Mrs O'Leary. "Good for nothing."

It is at this point – being compared to the father she's never met – that Trish realizes that her mother has been drinking. Which means that things are not going to get any better any time soon.

"Right," says Trish, calm as a stone. "I'm out of here. I'll see you back at the flat," and she turns round and marches back the short way they've just come.

Although not over-burdened with imagination, Trish does sometimes fantasize about having a different life. Especially when the one that she's in becomes so unpleasant. Trish's fantasies are almost always adventures involving pirates, spies, international thieves, or alien invaders. In these fantasies Trish not only SAVES THE DAY, but in doing so finally makes her mother happy.

Today, however, no fantasy comes to Trish's rescue. The parent-child relationship is, of course, a complex one, so although Trish knows that she's done nothing wrong she still feels guilty. When she gets back to the flat, she stands on the balcony, watching the road, waiting for her mother to return.

Trish stands on the balcony for over an hour,

but there is no sign of the ex-Mrs O'Leary making her way back home with a carrier bag of food for tea.

Trish hugs herself and bites her lip. Maybe she shouldn't have left her like that. There is no telling what might happen to her mother on her own in the state she's in. She once ended up in hospital with a broken arm. She has even been known – under the incredible stress of the half-term break – to disappear for a day or two.

Trish knows that if something dreadful has happened to her mother it will be her fault, and so she spends another thirty minutes thinking of reasons why it should take her mother so long to go round the corner to the shops. One of these reasons – that she didn't go to the shops but to the sad, old pub up the main road – is, of course, the right one.

There are a lot of ghosts about tonight, swarming through the gloomy night, but, as Trish watches the streets below, they aren't what she sees. What Trish sees is a world of loneliness and heartbreak that must be fought if any peace or happiness is ever to be won.

Thinking about her mother Trish, sighs. She goes back inside, puts on her jacket and leaves the flat for a second time.

Kiki Makes Himself Invisible

As Kiki's teachers have always been quick to say, Kiki is a very quiet boy. But (as they have been less quick to say) he is not a stupid one. He never goes straight home after school unless he has his bike with him, in case The Wat Boys are lying in wait – *three-forty-five, time to get the geek.* If he has his bike with him, Kiki knows that he can outrace and outmanoeuvre even The Wat Boys (who spend hours practising their wheelies, vaults and spins outside the block), but on foot he doesn't have a chance. Today, however, he doesn't have his bike with him because someone slashed his tyre when he was in the shop getting something for his mother last weekend. So Kiki makes his movements undependable, hard to predict – varying the route he takes and the time he gets back to The Wat. His mother thinks he goes home with friends, and is far too busy with his four little brothers and sisters to wonder why she never meets any of these friends. What Kiki really does is go to the library, which is not a place where he's ever likely to run into The Wat Boys. Today he has been even more cautious than usual, and it is almost dark by the time he comes in sight of Wat Tyler House. There are two reasons for this extra caution. The first is that he saw not one but two shooting stars from his bedroom window last night, which he knows is a warning of turmoil. The second is that, since it's the start of the half-term, The Wat Boys (whether they ever actually attend school or not) will be in a celebratory mood. At this time of year, a celebratory mood for The Wat Boys always involves bangers. The neighbourhood has sounded like a battlefield for days. If there's one thing worse than The Wat Boys, it's The Wat Boys armed.

Now Kiki comes round the corner, swinging his book bag over his shoulder, and stops, still as a rabbit who's just got a whiff of fox on the wind. This is always the most dangerous bit of the journey – which is why he's devised a complex arsenal of the rituals and charms taught to him by his grandmother to help him get through it.

Kiki stands at the corner, staring at the concrete tower he calls home. It is a long way from where he is to his flat on the sixteenth floor. He taps the roof of his mouth seven times with his tongue while he studies this distance. A bus has broken down, as buses sometimes do, so the traffic is barely moving, which is a bad thing. On the other hand, the pavement is crowded with people hurrying home, which is good. The bad thing about the traffic being stalled is that it means it will take Kiki longer to find three green cars than usual. The good thing about the busy pavement is that it shouldn't take him any time at all to find three people wearing something red. The colours are important. Since it's Friday, the three cars have to be green and the three people have to be wearing red, or the charm won't work.

Kiki spots a girl wearing a red scarf, a boy wearing a red baseball cap and a small child in a red jacket within five minutes, but it's another twenty minutes before the third green car finally appears. Then – and only then – can he start walking again, up the hill and into the road that leads to the tower blocks.

Not that the ritual ends there.

He can't look left or right. He can't step on any cracks. He can't smile at, wave at, or speak to anyone. He must repeat over and over a prayer that wards off evil. If he breaks any of these rules he won't be invisible any more. The prayers and the charms were taught to him by his grandmother when he lived where you could see the stars over your head at night like a tent. His ability to see ghosts is the reason she taught him the prayers and charms. Kiki is a gifted child.

And so it is that, looking neither left nor right, hopping and skipping over every crack, Kiki makes his way up the hill and along the road to Wat Tyler House, his fingers crossed so tightly that his knuckles turn white.

Sometimes the charms work. More than once, head down and the words of the prayer filling his mind, Kiki has walked right past The Wat Boys without being spotted. You might say that this was because they had their backs turned and were too involved in themselves to notice anyone else – but Kiki knows it was because he was invisible and, therefore, protected.

By rolling his eyes upwards without raising his head, Kiki can see several ghosts, moving through each other on their separate strands of time, and Trish O'Leary walking quickly towards him from Wat Tyler House, but there is no sign of The Wat Boys.

Then will I swim among the stars… Kiki silently recites – and, head still down and eyes now on the threatening cracks, starts to walk a little faster.

And then he hears them behind him.

"Oi! Look! It's the dirty gippo!" shouts one.

"Oi! gippo! We wanna talk to you!" shouts another.

A banger explodes in the road.

And sometimes, of course, the charm doesn't work and Kiki has to resort to more prosaic means of protection. On the prosaic level, humans have two possible responses to danger: fight or flight.

Kiki starts to run.

Help Comes from an Unexpected Source

Although Mr Chumbley thinks he knows everything there is to know about St Barnabas, he does not. For there is one thing about the church that neither Betty Friedman nor Sir Alistair Deuce has told him. This was not an oversight. The small, but important, detail that Betty Friedman and Sir Alistair failed to mention is that St Barnabas stands on a Time Portal. Through this Portal it is possible to leave the present and travel to the past as easily as getting on a bus and going into town. This is not, of course, something Mr Chumbley needs to know. Had they told him about the Time Portal, he would have laughed. Had they eventually managed to convince him, it would have done him no good. The Portal can only be opened by a very special few – by those who understand that the world is not just what you see, but what you don't see as well, in much the same way that the leaf is not the tree. Unlike Betty Friedman and Sir Alistair Deuce, this is not a group to which Mr Chumbley belongs. Despite his belief that his position in the Government makes him special, Mr Chumbley is just an ordinary man – and a very limited and mediocre one at that.

To one side of, and slightly behind, St Barnabas is a house that, like the church, has seen better centuries. This was the vicarage. Once upon a time there was always a light burning in the front window, a tumble of flowers in the gardens, and laughter sounding through the very walls. Now it is dark and still, surrounded by weeds and brambles, its pathways turned to rubble, its gardens thick and wild. It is here that Betty Friedman now stands, beneath the crumbling portico, Mrs Calabash, her cat, still in her arms. Mrs Calabash, exhausted from the afternoon's excitement, is sleeping; Betty Friedman is staring out at the shadowy night. She is wondering what to do.

When Betty Friedman told Mr Edward I. Chumbley that she had the documents in a safe place she was, as you know, not telling the truth. It would have been more accurate to say that while she hopes that the documents are in a safe place, she doesn't know where they are for certain. She does, however, know where they are meant to be.

Betty Friedman looks over towards St Barnabas, but what she sees is not the ruin that it now is but the church as it was the last time she saw it: the tended lawn, the clutch of gravestones, the flag-stone path that leads from the wrought iron gate of the churchyard to the entrance, the lighted lamp hanging over the double front door. The memory of that visit, locked away from her for so many years, has finally returned. She remembers that her name was Constance Moore, not Betty Friedman, and that she arrived through the Portal as usual and not in a cab (though she did have a cat). She remembers emerging in the lower crypt, as she always did. And she remembers taking a flower from the bunch she'd brought with her and laying it on the small, carved sarcophagus in the niche of the eastern wall, which is another thing she always did. Then she climbed the stairs to the church. St Barnabas itself wasn't the object of her visit – the object of her visit was in a corner of the church-yard – but as she passed the vestry she saw that the ancient strongbox, containing every record of the lives that had been lived here, was gone. She remembers vowing to get them back.

Betty Friedman turns to look straight ahead. The pavement and the asphalt-covered road are gone, as are the car park and the concrete towers. In their place is a large green that separates St

Barnabas from the cottages on its other side. Betty Friedman squints into the dark night, thickly patched with fog. She can just make out a girl in a blue dress hurrying over the dirt road that runs between the churchyard and the green, a large bundle wrapped in a shawl held tightly in her arms. The girl puts her hand to the wrought iron gate as the shadows shift around her, her eyes on the side of the church and the unlocked door that leads to the crypt.

Betty Friedman catches her breath, but she already knows that this is where her memory ends – not locked away, but forever lost. At least it's lost to her. No matter how hard she tries, she can't find it, can't pull it out of time's depthless ocean. She doesn't know if the girl in the blue dress made it into the church. Reaching the gate to hide her bundle in the church is the last thing the girl will ever remember – that and a sudden, overpowering sense of dread. Which means that those are the last things Betty Friedman remembers, too. As the memory stops, the dirt road, the tended lawn, the wrought iron gate and the girl in the blue dress all vanish, leaving her staring at the side of the ruined church. The door to the crypt is not only shut now but boarded up. The old lady sighs. This is where the hope comes in. She hopes that her inability to remember hiding the documents in the church doesn't mean that she didn't. If luck is with her and they are inside St Barnabas, she will need help to find them; bodies younger than hers and not afflicted with age and arthritis that can scrabble, crawl and climb. And if they aren't... Well, then she will need help just the same.

A banger goes off somewhere nearby, and Mrs Calabash opens her eyes and sits up straight in Betty Friedman's arms. Mrs Calabash watches the boy running towards them. Betty Friedman watches the girl who is coming from the opposite direction.

Trish is marching determinedly to the pub to look for her mother when she spots Kiki ahead of her, standing at the end of the road like a sleepwalker. Even before one of them shouts, "Oi! Look! It's the dirty gippo!", she sees The Wat Boys turn the corner behind him.

The Wat Boys are one of the many things Trish O'Leary doesn't fear at all. She has known Brendan Clocker, their self-appointed leader, for as long as she can remember, and she has never let him push her around – or even think about pushing her around. But Trish knows that Kiki is afraid of them – and she knows why. She knows whose precious trainers are rotting on top of the bus shelter.

And so, without a second thought, Trish starts to run in Kiki's direction, believing that her presence will somehow keep him from harm. She reaches him just past St Barnabas. The Wat Boys are right behind him, whooping like the ancient warriors who once called this land their own.

"Get out of the way, O'Leary!" shouts Brendan Clocker. "We don't like to hurt no girls!"

So that's the good news, then.

"Go jump in the canal!" Trish screams back. Without having anything that could possibly be mistaken for a plan, she stretches out her hand to grab hold of Kiki.

"I'm warning you!" Brendan stops to light another firecracker. "Get out of the bleedin' way!" And he lobs the banger over Trish and Kiki's heads.

Inspired by the actions of their leader, the other boys are pulling firecrackers from their jackets and grabbing for the lighter. Brendan starts moving again.

Trish is wondering what to do to avoid being hit by either a fist or an exploding banger when she hears someone who is definitely not a Wat Boy shout, "Quickly! Come in here!"

Trish turns to her left. An old lady she has never seen before is standing at the door of the house that belongs to St Barnabas. The door is open and a pale but welcoming light surrounds her like a halo.

Trish has lived all her life in The Wat, which makes eleven very long years. She knows, therefore, that, although it doesn't seem so now, the house is as derelict and uninhabited as the church. Indeed, they are both in such an appalling state that they've never even been squatted in. The only signs of life she has ever seen round either building are the weeds that grow from the roofs and the cracks in the walls, and the occasional rat or feral cat. Nonetheless, she tightens her grip on Kiki's arm and tries to pull him towards the open door.

"No!" Kiki pulls back. Not only does he know as well as Trish that no one lives in the house – or could – but he assumes that the old lady is one of the ghosts who haunt the church. He'd rather take his chances with The Wat Boys than with a ghost.

"Don't be daft," says Trish. "You want them to set you on fire or something? Is that what you want?" And she yanks him with such force that he has no choice but to stumble after her.

More whoops and explosions follow them as they run over the rubble that used to be a path-way.

The old lady steps aside allowing Trish and Kiki to rush over the threshold.

"Oi, you old witch!" scream The Wat Boys.

"We'll get you for this!"

The old lady has the vague and sugary smile of a television grandmother who can't remember where she left her glasses. "You ought to be more careful whom you threaten," she calls back. "If I really am a witch I might just turn you all into something more useful – like slugs."

And with that she firmly shuts the door.

Out of the Street and into the Past

Trish and Kiki come to a stop as soon as they're safely past the front door.

Kiki, for one, has no intention of going any further. He has his eyes closed and is hitting his tongue against the roof of his mouth and trying to remember a charm that would be right for the situation he now finds himself in – although he isn't really sure just what that situation is yet.

But, since one of the advantages of not having every waking moment dominated by terror is the ability to take an interest in things other than oneself, Trish is looking round with unconcealed curiosity.

They are in a small hall with three doors leading off it – one on either side, and one at the back – and a staircase to the next floor. The hall contains a large, ornately carved stand with hooks running down the frame, a mirror at the centre and a container for umbrellas and walking sticks at the base. A bowler hat and a large straw bonnet with a dotted white veil hang on the hooks of the stand, and there is a black umbrella and a frilly white parasol in the container. The light that seemed to surround the old lady like a halo is coming from an oil lamp that hangs on a chain from the ceiling. The house may look derelict and close to collapse on the outside, but inside it looks as if it's been done up recently. The walls and doors are freshly papered and painted, the tiles of the hall are pristine, the banister gleams with polish.

Trish gives a discreet sniff. Instead of the stink of damp and decay she was expecting, the air is filled with a scent that she can't identify but that is lavender. It might occur to Trish to wonder why she never saw the builders, decorators and cleaners coming in and out but, before she can, the old lady bolts the front door and turns to her and Kiki with a smile.

She is not quite like most of the old ladies who wheel their trolleys from The Wat to the shops on the main road and back again. True, she is as wrinkled and white-haired as they are, but the majority of them wear slacks or jeans and trainers or plimsolls, which this old lady doesn't. Instead, their saviour wears a long patchwork skirt, a multicoloured, handknit jumper and what look very much like combat boots.

She stares right at both of them at the same time. "Perhaps we should begin by introducing ourselves," she says. "I am Betty Friedman, but you may call me Betty." Her smile is so warm and pleasant that it is difficult to believe that only a few seconds ago she was threatening to turn The Wat Boys into slugs. "And you are?"

"I'm Trish," says Trish "and this here's—" Trish gives Kiki a nudge.

Kiki grips Trish's arm, but has been temporarily struck dumb by the bolting of the front door. To add to that woe, Betty Friedman, as solid as he and Trish, doesn't look like any ghost he's ever seen before – which must mean that she is a shaman or a witch. Kiki doesn't like the idea of giving his name to someone who is either a shaman or a witch in case it gives her power over him.

"Kiki," Trish fills in when he fails to speak. "This here's Kiki."

"How very nice to meet you," says Betty Friedman. "Why don't you come into the parlour? I've made us all a nice cup of tea. And some ginger biscuits like the ones I used to have in Düsseldorf."

Although Kiki and Trish have never actually spoken to one another before, the experience of running from The Wat Boys has already established a bond between them – and it is a bond that finding themselves locked in the vicarage with Betty Friedman is doing a lot to strengthen. They exchange a meaningful, conspiratorial look. Kiki's nails dig into Trish's arm.

"Thanks," says Trish politely, "but we've really got to be getting back. Our mothers—"

"*Your* mother is in The George," cuts in Betty Friedman, "and is likely to be there for quite some time. And Kiki's mother is far too busy to notice if he's a bit later than usual."

Kiki is too surprised by this announcement to respond, but Trish is too surprised not to.

"Oi!" she says. "How do you know about my mum?"

"It's a small world," says Betty Friedman. "That's how. Things get around." She walks over to the door on the right of the hallway. "In any case, I think if you were to take a peek out of the front window you would see that those boys are still outside. It might be wise to stay in here until they give up and leave."

Trish opens her mouth to ask if there is a way out at the back, but isn't given the chance. Betty Friedman has opened the door to the parlour and is ushering them in.

"Cor," says Trish.

"Coo," whispers Kiki.

Neither of them has ever seen a room that looks even remotely like Betty Friedman's parlour before. Not in real life at any rate. Kiki's family arrived in England with only a few precious possessions, and their flat is sparsely furnished from charity shops and the Salvation Army. Trish's mother bought their furniture on credit in a popular, cheap home furnishings shop (so although it will have fallen apart before it is ever paid for, it was very trendy when she got it), but what pictures and ornaments there were have long ago been broken in fits of alcoholic rage. In contrast to these minimalist and modern approaches to interior decoration, Betty Friedman favours the pack-it-in-and-make-certain-it's-really-old style. The Victorian furniture is oversized and fussy. The frames of the sofa and chairs are curved and carved, the bodies covered in velvets and brocades, and the arms and backs protected by rectangles and ovals of handmade lace. There are tables, tiered stands and glass-fronted cases laden with bric-a-brac and figurines. On the mantelpiece there is a stuffed owl with a mouse in its mouth under a glass cloche and a green glass ball with the shape of a mushroom, formed by bubbles, at its centre. An entire wall is taken up by wooden shelves crammed with leather-bound books. The other walls are elaborately papered and covered with pictures in gilded frames; the floor is covered in several heavy, intricately patterned rugs, and the window is draped in blue velvet.

As remarkable as all this is, what is even more remarkable to Kiki and Trish is the fact that there is no TV or DVD player; no light that doesn't come from oil lamps or candles.

"It's like stepping back in time," Trish whispers.

Or into a witch's den, thinks Kiki.

But even the lack of electricity and entertainment devices isn't the most remarkable thing about Betty Friedman's parlour.

At the back of the room stands a large, round table covered in a fancy cloth. There are four chairs placed around the table – on one of which a small, silver tabby cat, marked with dots rather than stripes, is sleeping soundly – and a teapot, three cups and saucers, a sugar bowl, a milk jug and a plate of biscuits on top of it.

"I don't get it," Trish blurts out. "It's like you was expecting us or something."

Betty Friedman ignores this statement. "Don't stand there dilly-dallying." She waves them forward. "The tea will get cold."

Kiki is so surprised he ventures out of his usual shell of shyness. "But how could you be expecting us when we didn't know we were coming?"

Betty Friedman shrugs in a vague way. This clearly isn't a question that deserves much thought. "Let's just say that I was expecting someone," she says. "And it's turned out to be you two, hasn't it? Which I'm certain you'll agree is the thing that matters."

"Only it doesn't make sense," says Trish. Trish is a girl who likes things to make sense.

Which is not a trait she has in common with their host.

"Not everything has to make sense," Betty Friedman informs her. "Some things just are. Now do stop lolling about in the hall and come and have your tea."

Trish looks over at Kiki and mouths the words, "Weird or what?"

Kiki tightens his grip on her arm even more.

And yet they obey Betty Friedman and stop lolling about in the hall, though this is more because they both feel as if something is pulling them into the parlour than because they think it's a particularly good idea.

Betty Friedman directs them to take a seat on either side of the peacefully sleeping cat.

"Now isn't this pleasant?" she asks, as she sits down between them, apparently oblivious to the fact that their faces are far from expressing pleasure. "There's nothing as calming after a stressful day as a nice cup of tea, don't you agree?" She reaches for the pot. "And though I can't speak for you, of course, I have to say that I have certainly had a most stressful day."

Neither Kiki nor Trish says anything; their day seems to be getting more stressful by the second.

"Please help yourselves to milk and sugar." Betty Friedman hands them each a brimming cup.

The tea dispensed, Betty Friedman passes round the pink glass cake plate of misshapen biscuits. They each take one – more out of politeness than enthusiasm, since neither of them has ever had a biscuit that didn't come from a packet before and they aren't convinced that they're actually edible.

Kiki, who is desperately tapping his tongue against the roof of his mouth, simply stares at his biscuit as though it might explode, but Trish bites cautiously into hers, and is immediately filled with thoughts of pine trees covered in snow and people speaking German. For some reason, the fact that the biscuit is actually delicious restores Trish's flagging courage and she says, "So how long've you been living here, then?"

Betty Friedman gives another vague shrug. "Oh ... not too long."

Trish takes another bite. "Only I didn't see no movers or nothing."

"Well, perhaps you were at school." Betty

Friedman slowly sips her tea. "You do go to school, don't you?"

"Course I go to school." Trish looks around the room as she chews. Beside her is a small table with a piecrust rim. There are several old photographs on the table: a large family sitting in a garden, two little girls in button-up shoes with bows in their hair, a bearded man in a bowler hat and a woman wearing a large straw hat with a veil standing at the door of this very same house when it had a lush garden in front rather than rubble and weeds. "But it would've taken them ages to get all this stuff in here. Maybe days."

Betty Friedman puts down her cup. "I'm afraid we don't really have time for idle chit-chat. Time – as I'm certain they've taught you in your school – is of the essence."

Kiki looks over at Trish. "What's that mean?"

"It means that we don't have any to waste, that's what it means," answers Betty Friedman. "I have something important I must discuss with you."

Trish and Kiki exchange a nervous look. "With us?"

Betty Friedman can even look both of them in the eyes when they are sitting on opposite sides of the table. "Do you see anyone else here to whom I might be speaking?"

"No," mumbles Kiki, who desperately wishes

that he did. Preferably someone who isn't a witch.

"But you don't even know us," Trish objects. "Why would you want to talk to us?"

"I must say you are the most argumentative sort of child." Betty Friedman is now looking only at Trish. "I do hope I haven't made a mistake in thinking that you can help me with my little problem."

"Little problem?" repeats Kiki. This is the first thing Betty Friedman has said that hasn't caused terror to tighten its hold on his heart. In Kiki's world, a little problem is as normal as biscuits in a packet. His mother is always having little problems: jars that need opening, fuses that need mending, things that need to be glued back together.

Trish, too, in whom confusion has been building at a steady pace since they entered the house, feels herself relax. Little problems are something she handles all the time – the ex-Mrs O'Leary's life being comprised of an endless series of them. She smiles. "No worries," says Trish. "My mum always needs me to help her. I'll give you a hand."

Kiki nods. The sooner they do, he reckons, the sooner they can leave. "Me, too."

Betty Friedman takes another sip of tea. "You haven't heard my little problem yet," she says.

Kiki and Trish Hear about Betty Friedman's Little Problem

As you and I already know, Betty Friedman's little problem has nothing to do with opening jars or mending fuses.

"Oh, no, no, no. No, you've misunderstood me." Betty Friedman puts her cup back in its saucer, which is blue and looks as if it was chipped from the sky. "It's nothing like that."

Trish wipes biscuit crumbs from her mouth with the embossed, linen serviette that Betty Friedman has so thoughtfully provided. "Well what is it, then?"

"Do have another." Betty Friedman passes her the pink glass plate. "The problem is that I have lost something that I need to find quite urgently."

"Well, that's what I said, isn't it?" Trish takes a larger biscuit than she did before. "My mum's always losing her keys and things like that."

"I'm certain that she is," says Betty Friedman.

Since Kiki is still crumbling his first biscuit, she puts the plate back down on the table. "But this is something far more important than keys."

This time when Trish bites into her biscuit she hears music. "You wouldn't say that if you was locked out of your flat," she says with the authority of experience.

"Perhaps not," Betty Friedman concedes, "but as you may have noticed, I am *not* locked out of my house. What I am is missing some exceedingly important documents. Documents that I need to get hold of as soon as possible – preferably sooner."

"You mean like your passport or your work permit?" Kiki's father often says that these are the only things he owns that anyone would want to steal.

"More important than that, even," says Betty Friedman. "These documents are irreplaceable."

"Then you should have kept them someplace really safe," says Kiki. His parents keep their passports and his father's work permit in a steel box at the back of the wardrobe – hidden from thieves but easily retrieved should the flat catch on fire.

"Cups, please." Betty Friedman pours them all more tea. "As it happens, young Mr Monjate, that is precisely what I did." It is certainly what she had intended to do. "Unfortunately, that was some time ago, and now—"

"You can't remember where you put them?" offers Trish.

Betty Friedman's smile shows signs of strain. "It's very kind of you to try to shoulder some of the burden of this conversation, Trish, but that isn't what I was about to say at all." She picks up the cow-shaped jug and pours some milk into her tea. "As it happens, what I was about to say is that, although I know where they ought to be, I can't get at them." She slowly stirs her tea with a silver spoon, the handle of which is embossed with the head of an angel. "Without your help, that is."

"How come?" Trish eyes the biscuits, wondering if she dare help herself to another. "Where did you put them?"

"They're meant to be in St Barnabas. In the crypt."

Kiki stops tapping the roof of his mouth and frowns. "What's a crypt?"

"That's the basement. It's where they buried people who were too important to just go in the ground like everyone else," explains Trish.

"As it happens, the crypt I mean is far older than the church and actually *under* the basement of St Barnabas."

"And how're we meant to get down there?" asks Trish. "Dig a tunnel?"

"I doubt that will be necessary," Betty Friedman assures her. "There is a hidden trapdoor in the floor of St Barnabas' crypt, and beneath it, a stairway leading to the older crypt. The documents are there. There's a child's sarcophagus in the crypt. In a niche in the eastern wall. The documents are inside."

Kiki's spoon falls to the carpet with a thud. It is likely that there is more than one child buried under the church, but Kiki knows that even if there were a hundred, she is talking about the child he has seen being carried by the procession of ghosts.

Betty Friedman picks up the spoon and hands it to Kiki with an encouraging smile. "It's all right, you know. You shan't have to see the remains. The shroud is still intact."

Unable to decide which upsets him more – that he has seen the child's corpse or that the old lady knows that he has seen it – Kiki stares down at the heap of crumbs on his plate to avoid her eyes.

Betty Friedman sits back in her chair. "So you can appreciate my problem," she continues. "I'm far too old and arthritic to go rooting about in all that ruin and debris."

"Well, we're too young." says Trish. "We'll get one of those ASBOs if the coppers catch us trespassing."

"And when have you seen an officer of the law around here?" asks Betty Friedman. "Not that they'd notice you even if they did wander onto the estate. But an old woman poking round the church would be noticed."

"So what if they saw you?" Trish wants to know. "They'd just think you was looking for your cat."

"Perhaps," says Betty Friedman. "But perhaps not. To be honest, there is someone I'd rather didn't see me skulking about St Barnabas. He'll know precisely why I'm there."

"You make it sound like someone's after you." Trish sniggers. The only person likely to be after someone as old as Betty Friedman is the Grim Reaper.

"That may be because someone is." Betty Friedman rubs one finger round the rim of her saucer. "But he won't be expecting children. He won't think anything of seeing a couple of children."

"He will if the children are carrying crowbars," says Trish, who may have more imagination than I've previously given her credit for. " 'Cos that's the only way we could get in there. It's all boarded up. With metal and all."

"Where there's a will, there's a way," says Betty Friedman, as though this settles the matter. "I'm certain you'll get in without too much trouble."

"And what about the rats?" counters Trish. She doesn't fancy hanging out with rats.

And the ghosts… Kiki watches the last vestige of his ginger biscuit fall onto his plate.

"You may take Mrs Calabash with you." Betty Friedman gestures to the cat, who heretofore has given no sign of ever waking up. "The rats won't bother you. She'll put them off. And the ghosts won't bother you, either. As I do believe you already know, Kiki, they're not out to harm anyone, they're simply caught in time."

Kiki isn't too happy that Betty Friedman seems to know his thoughts, which makes him, if not as argumentative as Trish, rather more querulous than usual. "But what if the documents aren't there any more?" He risks a glance in Betty Friedman's direction. "You know, if they were put there so long ago, maybe somebody's taken them."

Instead of saying, "*Of course they're there*," as he expects her to, Betty Friedman says, "Unfortunately, that is a distinct possibility." She fiddles absentmindedly with the wooden button on her jumper. "Not that someone else has taken them, of course – that would be impossible – but that I – that the person who was meant to hide them never managed to complete the task. I simply can't be certain." Betty Friedman sighs. "If that is the case, I shall have to find a way of getting into the crypt myself after all."

"What's the point of that if the documents ain't there?" demands Trish.

"If they aren't there, then I shall have to go back in time to find them, that's what the point is."

Trish assumes this must be some weird old-lady sort of joke, and snorts with laughter. "Yeah, right."

"How delightful is the sound of childish laughter," murmurs Betty Friedman. "But, as it happens, Trish O'Leary, St Barnabas stands – insofar as it can be said still to stand – on sacred land. It has always been a place where the boundaries of time are thin enough to pass through."

Trish gives another derisive laugh. "You what?"

Kiki, however, knows exactly what the old lady is talking about. "But I thought that just because you've got a Portal you're still not meant to interfere with the past."

Betty Friedman turns to him. "Technically you're not," she says. "Certainly, ordinary people mustn't interfere. But for people like myself there is leeway. Of course, one can't do anything that would change events, but retrieving something that's been left behind for a good cause is an entirely different matter."

Trish, however, is still thinking about boundaries of time that are thin enough to pass through. She looks over at Kiki. "What's she on about?"

"There's a Portal under the church." Kiki's grandmother taught him all about Portals, of course. Seers and shamans use them to move through realities, which is why they understand the nature of the universe and what's truly important in life. "You know, it's an entrance to other dimensions. A Portal through time."

The only thing Trish's grandmother ever taught her was not to wear her Wellies in the house or she'd go blind. Trish looks from Kiki to Betty Friedman, and back. "You what?" She laughs again, although now there is a nervousness in her voice that even she can hear. "That's rubbish. People can't travel through time."

"No," agrees Betty Friedman. "Not most people. But I can. Within reason, of course. I can't go into the future, but I can certainly go back to the past."

The old lady is obviously even madder than Trish thought. And because she is so mad – and, therefore, possibly dangerous – Trish beats back the impulse to say, "You mean on your flippin' broomstick?"

"And, no, it's not because I'm a witch, or a shaman," snaps Betty Friedman.

Trish kicks her heels against the rung of her chair. "I didn't say nothing," she grumbles.

Kiki is staring down at the plate of crumbs as though he would like very much to put his face in it, but manages to mumble, "So what are you, then?"

"Oh, I've been called many things in my time," she answers, not mentioning that witch and shaman are two of those many things. "But I like to think of myself as a Time Keeper."

Trish, frowns. "What's that mean then?"

"A Time Keeper remembers what others have long forgotten," Betty Friedman explains. "A Time Keeper is dedicated to the ever-present past and to keeping it in living memory."

What she is, thinks Trish, is mad as about a hundred hatters. As a girl who spends a great deal of time in front of the telly, Trish knows from programmes she's seen that people who are truly mad often hear voices or think they're King Arthur or someone like that. Someone like a Time Keeper.

"The past's not ever-present. It's *gone*," argues Trish. "That's why they call it the past, ain't it?"

"It may be gone to you, Trish O'Leary, but let me assure you that your misguided opinion doesn't affect the nature of the cosmos in the least." Betty Friedman sighs. "I can see that I'm going to have to tell you everything." Or, if not every single thing, then quite a lot of them. "Let's start with my documents, shall we?" She pushes her cup away from her.

It looks as if this could be a long story. Trish helps herself to another biscuit. Kiki puts his hands on his lap and crosses every finger.

"The documents record the history of the land on which St Barnabas stands. It has been a place of enormous cultural and historical significance for thousands of years, and by all rights should be made into a World Heritage Site."

"But it ain't, is it?" Trish interrupts once more. "It's going to be turned into posh flats." She bites into the biscuit, and smells snow. "My mum thinks that'll be better. She says the church is an eyesore."

"Does she?" Betty Friedman squeezes her lips together as though about to spit out an apple pip. "Your mother also thinks that getting blotto in The George is going to make her happy. She's wrong about that, and she's wrong about this. St Barnabas is important and all the priceless arte-facts that lie beneath it are also immeasurably important because they are links to the past."

"Artefacts?" Trish sounds slightly sneering. "You mean like old swords and coins and stuff like that?" Trish has seen several TV programmes about blokes with metal detectors discovering old swords and coins and stuff like that, but it isn't something she associates with where she lives. She associates drink cans and burger boxes with where she lives.

Betty Friedman nods. "Precisely. Weapons ... tools ... jewellery ... There's a veritable treasure trove under the church. But what is even more important is the land it's on. The land is a living thing, just like you and I. But, unlike you and I, who are only passing through as it were, it is an ultimate reality."

Only by biting her lip does Trish manage not to laugh again.

Though this doesn't stop Betty Friedman from glaring at her as if she has not only laughed but spat crumbs all over the table. "And what about you, Kiki?" Betty Friedman turns to him. "What do you think?"

It is such an unusual occurrence for anyone to ask Kiki's opinion about anything that he is surprised into answering. "My mum thinks it's a good thing, too. You know, because there's bound to be jobs going." As if Mrs Monjate doesn't have enough to do, she also works as a cleaner.

"I do understand that your family needs the money, but that is a very short-term view, if I may say so," says Betty Friedman. "Your mother and everyone else will be far better off with a World

Heritage Site on their doorstep than a block full of people who can't clean their own flats. And, in any event, I didn't ask what your mother thinks, I asked what you think."

Kiki shrugs. "Well... I reckon with the ghosts and all ... you know, if it really is a Portal ... I mean, you shouldn't mess with things like that."

"Precisely." Betty Friedman nods approvingly for a change. "One shouldn't mess with things like that."

Although Trish suspects that logic works no better with mad, old women than it does with her mother, her practical mind feels it has to try. "Why don't you just go to the Council or whatever and tell them about the historical significance and all?"

Betty Friedman cocks her head as though studying Trish. "You're quite a clever girl, aren't you? But, fortunately, my survival over the centuries hasn't depended on having your advice. As it happens, I have already spoken to two of the councillors. That's why it's so exceedingly important that I find those documents. If I can produce proof of the importance of the site by the Council meeting on Tuesday afternoon, then St Barnabas will be saved. If not, the property will be sold and they'll be knocking it down by Wednesday morning."

"Why did you wait till the last minute, then?" ventures Kiki. "Why didn't you try to stop them before?"

"I've been extremely busy, haven't I?" Betty Friedman retorts. "I don't think you appreciate how difficult my job is. There's always far too much to do – especially nowadays when everything's changing and moving so swiftly. I can't be everywhere at once, you know. And it does happen that, despite one's best intentions, time just slips away."

"What about the bloke who's buying it?" asks the ever-practical Trish. "Maybe if you talked to him—"

"Talk to him?" This is the first time they've heard Betty Friedman laugh; it is a sound that, were it a fruit, would be a lemon. "Ah..." breathes Betty Friedman. "Now we've come to the other part of my little problem."

Almost against his will Kiki hears himself whisper, "You mean the man who's after you, right?"

Betty Friedman nods. "The very same." She picks up a large, over-full carpetbag from the floor beside her chair, opens it and pulls out a small stack of clippings from somewhere inside it. "Here." She hands some of the clippings to Kiki and the rest to Trish.

The pictures are of an imposing looking man of

the sort never seen round The Wat except on a TV screen. In the photographs he is sometimes alone and sometimes with someone just as imposing, but he is always wearing an immaculate dark suit and a you-can-trust-me smile. The pictures are all different, but all the same.

"He looks well posh," says Trish.

Betty Freedman gives her a very small and very fleeting smile. "He is 'well posh', as you so charmingly put it. His name is Sir Alistair Deuce."

"He must be important," says Kiki. "There's one of him shaking hands with the Prime Minister."

"He'll shake hands with anyone," Betty Friedman tells him. "But, yes, he is important. Very important. He is one of the wealthiest men in the world."

"What's he do?" Trish stares at a photo of Sir Alistair that seems to have been taken right in front of the church next door. "He don't look like a film star or nothing like that."

"That is very probably because he isn't. Far from it. Film stars are paid a great deal of money to do very little, while Sir Alistair is paid a great deal of money to destroy very much."

Trish lays the clippings on the table. "You mean like some kind of terrorist?"

"I mean like a property developer."

Just about the only thing that Trish O'Leary will ever have in common with Mr Edward I. Chumbley is that she also thinks the odds against someone like Betty Friedman being involved with someone like Sir Alistair Deuce are fairly high. "But why's he after *you*?"

"Do you want the short, simple answer – or the longer, more complicated one?"

"The short, simple one," Kiki and Trish answer together. They both are feeling that they would very much like to go home.

"Very well," says Betty Friedman. "The short, simple answer is that Sir Alistair owns the Futures Development Corporation, Ltd, and has made a deal with the Government to buy St Barnabas and turn it into luxury flats. Obviously, Sir Alistair stands to make a great deal of money from this deal. Less obviously, he stands to make millions – possibly billions – more, because Sir Alistair knows that buried under the church is a treasure trove of rare and ancient artefacts of incalculable value. And that, of course, is one of the things he's really after—"

"But they don't belong to him," interrupts Trish. "I saw this programme on the telly and they said you have to hand over anything like that that you find. That's the law."

Betty Friedman shakes her head. "As if that

would stop Sir Alistair. Men such as he believe that laws exist only for other people." She takes the top picture from Trish's pile and looks at it almost wistfully. "You wouldn't think to look at him now, but he used to have great promise. Very great promise. He could even once have been a High King."

Trish isn't sure what a High King is, but it sounds to her like someone who would SAVE THE DAY. It definitely sounds a lot better than a property developer. "What happened?"

"I'm afraid that most of us find it far easier to do things for money than for love." Betty Friedman sighs, also almost wistfully. "What happened to him is what often happens. Power went to his head."

Trish, with her practical mind, has been listening to the facts of Betty Friedman's story, but Kiki, with his intuitive mind, has been listening to what lies beneath them – much in the way that the artefacts lie under the old church next door. Now (and, once again, almost against his will) he says, "Is Sir Alistair a Time Keeper, too?"

"How very perceptive of you, Kiki Monjate." It isn't often that Betty Friedman shows any surprise. "Indeed, he *was*." Betty Friedman's eyes are still on the photograph, but it is clear, at least to Kiki, that she is looking at something else – something long ago and far away. "Now he is something else entirely. He likes to call himself a Renegade Time Keeper, but what he actually is, is a destroyer of time. Which is the other reason he wants St Barnabas – so he can close off the Portal. The fewer Portals, you see, the more difficult it is for we true Time Keepers to do our job." She sighs again, and now, when she looks up, she is back in the present and seeing only them. "Well," she says, "do I have your help?"

"But don't you need someone ... you know, with special powers or something?" asks Trish. "Why pick us?"

Betty Friedman raises one eyebrow. "Why not? Kiki understands the vastness and complexity of the universe, and although you like to think of yourself as being as practical as boots in the rain, you are actually a girl with a very generous spirit and an independent mind. These are qualities that give you both more power than you realize. Besides, it is about time that both of you started to take some initiative in your lives. You can't simply let things happen to you, you have to participate." Betty Friedman's eyes don't leave theirs. "So, do I hear a yes or a no?"

Kiki looks at Trish.

Trish clears her throat. "I'm sorry, Miss—"

"Betty," corrects her host.

"I'm sorry, Betty," says Trish. "It's just that … I mean … don't you think you're being a little … a little paranoid?" Trish is very familiar with the concept of paranoia because it's one of the things her mother gets when she's wound herself up on unhappiness or red wine.

"Are you saying that you don't believe me?"

Trish shifts uneasily in her chair. "I'm not saying you're lying or nothing."

"You think I'm just a gaga, old lady."

Since this is exactly what Trish does think she says, "No, of course I don't. But it's all a bit hard to believe ain't it? You know, that somebody like this Sir geezer would be after you and all."

"And what about you, Kiki?" asks Betty Friedman. "Do you think I'm just a gaga old lady, too?"

If only… thinks Kiki.

"No." He shakes his head. "I don't think that." Which he certainly doesn't. "And I'd like to help. Really. But my mum … you know … she needs me … and, you know, she wouldn't want me to do anything dangerous."

"I see. Well that's settled, then." Betty Friedman sounds so reasonable, that anyone would think that she's a person who regularly takes "no" for an answer – which she isn't. What she is, however, is a person who knows that there is more than one way to cook an egg – or, in this case, more than one way to get someone to help you when they really would rather not. She pushes back her chair. "Goodness me!" she cries, her eyes all at once on the grandfather clock in the corner. "Will you look at the time? You'll want to be going home – now that the coast is clear." She reaches into her bag again and removes a small photograph. "I'd like you to take this." She thrusts the photograph into Trish's hand. "Something to remember me by."

As if they are likely to forget her.

"That's all right," says Trish. "You don't have to give us nothing."

"Oh, but I insist," says Betty Friedman. "I really must insist. Put it in your pocket, and be sure to keep it safe."

Somehow, without either Trish or Kiki knowing how it happened, they find themselves out of the parlour and standing at the open front door.

"Now get on home," says Betty Friedman. "And promise me you'll look after yourselves."

"We will," says Trish.

"Thank you for the tea and biscuits," says Kiki.

But Betty Friedman doesn't hear them. She has already shut the door.

Trish and Kiki Have a Difference of Opinion

Trish and Kiki stand on the doorstep of the vicarage for a few seconds, looking over at The Wat, both somewhat stunned, in their different ways, by their encounter with Betty Friedman.

Trish is thinking that, with the windows all lit up and the satellite dishes on the roof, The Wat not only looks strange and exotic, but as if it's about to take off. "It don't look real somehow," she says. Although it has never looked like this to her before and she doesn't know why it should look that way now. "You know, like it's on some other planet."

This, of course, is not what Kiki was thinking – it's not even close. Kiki was thinking about his grandmother. Kiki's grandmother believed in the old ways. She believed that there is more in the universe than the everyday things we see around us. Other realities; greater truths. She wouldn't have been surprised or frightened by Betty Friedman or her house or her request for help. Kiki's grandmother said that when Kiki was born she saw a sign that he was one who would carry the old ways into the future. That's why she taught him everything she knew. Now Kiki is wondering if that's why Betty Friedman plucked him off the street – because she knows that his grandmother saw a sign. She seems to know everything else about him. He gives himself a shake. "If you want to know what I think, I think we're the ones who've been on another planet." The planet Betty Friedman. "Let's just get out of here."

"Like I want to hang around, right?" Trish starts to walk quite quickly towards the tower blocks of home. "And if you want to know what *I* think, I think the old lady's barking mad. I'm going home to watch telly and forget about the whole thing."

Since Kiki had a grandmother who believed in worlds that can't be seen, his opinion of Betty Friedman's sanity is not the same as Trish's, of course. Normally, he wouldn't mention this. He has learned (the hard way) that it's easier to get on with people if you agree with them. There has been nothing normal about the afternoon, however, and now he says, "But what if she isn't?"

Trish looks over at him, trotting beside her to

keep up. "What do you mean, 'What if she isn't?' Are you joking? Time Keepers and time travel and friends of the Prime Minister chasing after her like they're gangsters...? She's practically howling at the moon."

"Yeah ... but ... you know ... it was pretty strange, wasn't it? You know, her being there and all."

Trish's only reply is to give him a withering look.

Kiki takes a deep breath and goes on. "I think that maybe we should've asked for the long, complicated explanation. I mean, how come she had the tea all ready like that? And she knew our last names and about our mums. And when did she move in? You didn't see anyone moving in, and neither did I. Nobody ever goes near the church because it's such a tip, but the house wasn't a tip inside, was it? It was all done up proper."

Trish knows perfectly well that none of the things Kiki mentioned make any sense at all, but for once this isn't a problem for her. She doesn't want to make sense out of what happened; she simply wants it to go away.

"Well, I dunno, do I?" Trish walks a little faster. "Maybe she had it all done up while we was at school. And that's when she moved in, too. When we was at school."

"You said yourself that it would've taken hours to get all that stuff inside," Kiki reminds her. "And it would've taken weeks to do it up. There's no way she could've done all that without somebody noticing. It would've been all over The Wat in minutes. We would've heard about it."

"Maybe not." Trish opens the door to the block and strides inside. "She could've moved in with nobody knowing. It's possible." *If she did it by some sort of magic*, whispers a tiny voice deep in her mind. But it is a voice to which Trish also refuses to listen. "The old boy next to us died and new people moved in and we didn't have a clue for months."

Kiki, however, seems suddenly determined to make up for all the arguments he's avoided in his life. "Well, what about the tea?" He follows Trish into the foyer, a place that has been compared unfavourably to the waiting room of hell by more than one of its occupants. "And knowing about our names and our mums and all?"

"She probably makes tea like that every afternoon even though nobody ever comes. That's the sort of thing mad people do." Trish steps gingerly into the lift – partly to avoid stepping in pee and partly because riding the lifts of Wat Tyler House requires a certain amount of courage as well as faith. "And as for our mums, she's probably seen them round the estate."

"She knew our last names," repeats Kiki. He starts moving the fingers of his right hand very rapidly to prevent the lift from getting stuck between floors. "How did she know them? We didn't tell her what they were."

Trish pushes the button for her floor. "Mad people just know things. Like those blokes who can hardly talk but who can add hundreds of numbers in their heads."

"You know what I think?" Kiki has to stand on tiptoe to hit the button for the sixteenth floor. "I think she really is what she says. You know, a Time Keeper. She's definitely some sort of witch. She's got a cat. All witches have cats."

The lift always makes a heavy, grinding noise as it starts to rise – something Kiki finds extremely unnerving – but this time he doesn't hear it because Trish is laughing so much.

"Some sort of witch?" she hoots. "Are you for real? Lots of people have a cat. And anyway, there's no such thing as witches, you berk. That's just stories. And no such thing as a Time Keeper, neither. Unless it's a clock."

"In my country we believe in things like that," says Kiki.

Trish steps away from a suspicious puddle in the corner. "Yeah, well we ain't in your country, are we? We're in England."

"That doesn't mean there aren't any spirits or witches or things like that," says Kiki. "And what about that glass ball on the mantelpiece? That looked like a crystal ball to me. Spirits like glass because they can see out."

Trish slaps her forehead in mock-astonishment. "Oh, of course! That must be what that ghost is doing in our washing machine!"

"You shouldn't make fun," warns Kiki. "If Betty Freedman has got powers—"

"The only power she's got is the power of the law. *If* she finds those documents." Trish removes the photograph the old lady gave them from her pocket. "What do you think we should do with this?"

"She said to keep it safe," says Kiki. "So I reckon that's what you should do."

Trish looks down at the photograph, seeing it for the first time. It is a picture of St Barnabas, taken so long ago that a wrought iron fence still encircles it and the headstones all stand in rows. Given its age, it is in remarkably good condition –the image strong and clear, and neither faded, nor cracked by time. Trish squints at the photograph in the gloomy, unenthusiastic light of the lift. As she watches, what at first like looked shrubs and shadows seem to change into men in top hats and women in bonnets, all standing in a group with the vicar in the centre in front of the open door of the church. It's all Kiki's stupid talk about witches, she knows, but she suddenly decides that she'd much rather not have the picture in her room with her. She holds the photo out to him. "Why don't you take it?"

Kiki, however, doesn't reach for it. "Why don't you? You're the one she gave it to."

"She gave it to both of us."

He moves back as the lift finally stops at Trish's floor with a moan and a rattle. "Well, it wouldn't be safe at mine." The doors creak open. "Not with my brothers and sisters."

This isn't the first time Trish has wished she wasn't an only child. "But there must be some-place—"

"No, really." Kiki takes another step backwards. "They get at everything."

Trish looks down at the picture as she steps into the hall.

"Well, see you," says Kiki.

It almost seems as though the people who have inexplicably appeared in the picture are moving about.

"Yeah," says Trish. "See you around."

Trish Has a Dream

As soon as Trish gets in the flat, she goes to her room and puts the picture under her mattress, where it will be both safe and out of her sight. Then she gets herself a sandwich, a drink and a packet of crisps, and settles down to watch the telly. Betty Friedman may not have special powers as far as Trish is concerned, but the telly does. Through the miracle of television, Trish can forget that she is just a lonely little girl with a difficult mother in a sad little flat with a terrific view of the motorway, and be part of worlds she couldn't imagine by herself. Such are its magical effects that they very soon put the strange, old woman and the strange afternoon completely out of her mind. They also put her mother out of her mind until the film she's been watching ends. It's nearly ten at night. Trish goes out on the balcony to see if there is any sign of the ex-Mrs O'Leary weaving her way back home, but the road below is empty and dark. As is the house hunched in the shadows on the other side of the road. Old ladies go to bed early, Trish tells herself. And after spending hours in the pub her mother probably won't go to bed at all. So she might as well go to bed herself.

Trish steps back inside, and takes her glass and sandwich plate into the kitchen to clean them and put them in the rack to dry. If her mother does come home, a dirty plate and glass left on the coffee table will only set her off.

When Trish returns to the sitting room the news is on. This is not a programme she usually watches. Trish is about to turn off the set when she realizes that she is staring into the shining smile of none other than Sir Alistair Deuce himself. His voice moves as smoothly over each syllable he speaks as a snake slithers over the ground.

"Blimey!" mutters Trish, and plops back onto the sofa as though she's been dropped.

Sir Alistair has been appointed Chairman of a special committee to advise the government on development. "The past is gone," says Sir Alistair Deuce. "The landscape and architecture it produced are antipathetic to the way we live now. We, as a nation, must look forward. We must create living environments and transport infrastructures that are high-functioning, efficient and sustain-able."

Trish doesn't understand half of what he is saying (and that half is largely the small words like "the" and "is"), but she gets the gist. Sir Alistair clearly feels that it is time we stopped being sentimental about old trees (that are going to die anyway) and old buildings (that should have been torn down years ago), and started again with everything new. She stares at the handsome, relentlessly smiling, well-groomed figure on the box, wondering if he is capable of harming an old lady. His ice-cap eyes stare back at her. Trish decides that he is. It's not my problem, she tells herself, and switches off the set.

Trish leaves the light on in the hall and doesn't put the chain on the door, in case her mother comes home, and goes to her room.

That night she has a dream.

Trish has two recurring dreams. The first is about winning the lottery and being able to buy her mother everything she's ever wanted. The second is that she and her mother are reunited with her father, who isn't a cab driver, as she's been told, but the king of a small, vaguely European country who takes them to live in his palace by the sea. In either case, everyone lives happily ever after and Trish always wakes up in a good mood.

This dream is nothing like either of those.

Trish dreams that she is standing in front of St Barnabas. But it isn't St Barnabas as she knows it. Instead of the bottles and McDonald's containers, wildflowers cover the ground. The steps to the church aren't broken or overgrown with weeds and the headstones in the cemetery haven't toppled over. The door is bright with paint and open wide, the stained glass windows shine with stories told in rainbows. There are people milling around her, chatting and smiling, but Trish is the only one dressed in jeans and trainers and a Nike T-shirt. The others are the people from the photograph – all dressed in their Sunday best. In her dream, Trish is looking for someone, though she doesn't know for whom. Her eyes search for something familiar – something that will tell her why she's having this particular dream – but the road and the car park and the tower blocks are all gone, of course, and in their place is a large green and a clutch of cottages. Trish leaves the group at the front of the church and goes round to the side of the building. She opens the door that leads to the crypt, but instead of stepping through it she suddenly turns round. Everything has changed. The smiling people are gone and a still, ominous darkness has descended, clotted with dense fog. Trish squints into the gloom. A girl in a blue dress is hurrying over the dirt road that runs between the churchyard and the green, a large bundle wrapped in a shawl held tightly in her arms. Despite the dark and the swirling fog Trish can see the girl clearly – her copper-coloured hair and sea-green eyes, both of which seem to burn in the night. Now Trish can hear her footsteps – urgent as fear – and behind them a heavier, determined tread and, behind those, still well in the distance, hoof beats. The girl puts her hand to the wrought iron gate at the front of the church as the shadows shift around her. Trish is about to call out a greeting when a man suddenly materializes out of the fog behind the young woman. He is dressed all in black, his collar up, a slouch hat pulled low on his forehead, obscuring his face. "Oi!" shouts Trish. "Oi! Look round!" But the young woman doesn't seem to hear her. Trish opens her mouth to warn her again, but before she can speak the man grabs the girl in blue, dragging her back from the gate and wrenching her hand from its glove, which falls to the ground like a dead leaf. Trish screams, which is the thing that finally wakes her up.

She sits up in bed, her heart pounding. Dawn is breaking over Wat Tyler House, making her room shadowy and grey.

It was just a dream, Trish tells herself. Because of that mad old woman and weird Kiki with his witches and spirits and all.

Nonetheless, she reaches under the mattress and pulls out the picture. It isn't exactly the same picture that it was the night before. It is St Barnabas, as once it was, but the door is shut and there is definitely no one standing in front of the church now. Trish rubs the sleep from her eyes and stares hard at the image. She can just make out a glove on the ground by the gate.

Trish and Kiki
Go for a Walk

Kiki sits on the edge of his bed in his underwear, one plain black sock dangling from his hands. He has been sitting like this for the past twenty minutes, trying to make the thoughts that have been tearing through his mind like tiny tornadoes since yesterday quieten down enough for him to get dressed. He moves his hand, and watches the shadow of the sock sway across the tiles of the floor like a demon swooping low in the sky. What if the demon comes after him? What if, even as he sits here in the cramped room he shares with his two brothers, with the picture of his grandmother taped to the wall above his bed, the demon is gliding towards him, swift and soundless as a snake? He knows the demon; why shouldn't the demon know him?

Kiki had trouble sleeping last night. As certain as Trish is that Betty Friedman is just a mad old woman, Kiki is certain that she's exactly what she claims; a Time Keeper – a shaman on an endless quest. Long after his brothers were fast asleep in the bunk beds on the other side of the room, Kiki lay awake, staring up at the patterns of light on the ceiling. Of all the things to worry about in England, Kiki never expected that having a shaman as a neighbour would be one of them.

Finally, he slipped from his bed and went into the kitchen to make himself a cup of what his grandmother always called "calming" tea. His father wasn't home yet, and his mother was dozing in front of the telly. He tiptoed past her. It was as he was on his way back to bed that he heard a voice that immediately destroyed all the good done by the tea. Not that the voice was shrill or shouting. Not that it threatened or thundered. Indeed, it was a well-modulated, persuasive and soothing voice, but Kiki recognized it at once as the voice of someone bent on betrayal and destruction. His heart racing, he looked over to see to whom the voice belonged. There on the telly was the man Betty Friedman had told them about; Sir Alistair Deuce. As he stood there – Sir Alistair's voice cutting through his soul likes knives and his cold, blue, depthless eyes seeming to bore into his own – Kiki knew that, though he might call himself a Renegade Time Keeper, Sir Alistair was really something else. The word ran up his spine like electricity running up a wire. Demon. Not the demons of old with horns and tails and crocodile teeth. A modern demon in a dark grey suit and a brightly striped, silk tie – smiling as if he owned the world.

Kiki is still watching the shadow of the sock when the bedroom door suddenly bursts open. He jumps and turns sharply, half-expecting to see Sir Alistair Deuce in the doorway, looking right at him.

But it is only Kiki's mother, looking fraught – though this, of course, is not an unusual state for her to be in. She has what appears to be cereal in her hair and the baby in her arms. "Kiki! Whatever is the matter with you? I've been calling and calling!"

"I—"

"And look at you! You're not even dressed."

"I—"

"You had better put some clothes on." His mother removes a small fist from her eye. "Your friend is here for you."

Kiki is still thinking of Sir Alistair Deuce. "My friend?"

"She's in the hallway," says his mother. "She didn't want to come in."

* * *

Trish wants to talk, which is not something that can be done easily in the Monjate household without shouting. If this were any other day, Kiki would have refused to leave the flat without the protection of his mother and brothers and sisters, but it's a Saturday, and he knows that on Saturdays The Wat Boys take out their aggression on the football field over at the recreation grounds. Besides, if he doesn't talk to someone about his fears he may implode. Talking about Kiki's fears is another thing that doesn't get done in the Monjate household; his mother has enough to worry about.

Although they don't discuss it, both Trish and Kiki automatically turn left when they leave the building – in the opposite direction from Betty Friedman's house.

While they walk, Trish tells Kiki about her dream and the things that she saw in the photograph.

"It was well weird," she says in summation.

What Trish has described is, of course, the sort of thing that Kiki sees and dreams all of the time – without any outside help – but he decides against mentioning this to Trish. She already thinks that he's strange enough.

Nonetheless, he can't keep a small amount of triumph from his voice. "Didn't I say Betty

Friedman's got powers?" he demands. "Didn't I say there's more going on than she said? Maybe you believe me now."

Trish looks at him as though she hasn't truly seen him before. "You're bonkers, too, aren't you?" Although she is still upset, daylight has done a great deal to restore Trish's confidence in logic and reason. "I reckon it's not just an ordinary photograph. I reckon it's got some sort of hologram thing on it. You know, like those pencil cases where if you move it you see different pictures." This is the rather ingenious explanation that Trish has come up with, and she's reasonably happy with it. It is certainly far better than the other possible explanation, which is that the photograph does actually change.

But Kiki isn't happy with this at all. "I don't think that's possible," he says. "The hologram can't be part of the photograph, it'd have to be stuck on. So you'd be able to see it. You could just peel it off."

Trish gives him a scornful look. "Maybe you haven't twigged yet, Kiki, but for everyone else this is the twenty-first century. Science can do absolutely anything nowadays. They said so on the telly."

"Then what about your dream?" he persists. "You said what you saw in your dream was like what you saw in the photo. That's not a hologram thingy, is it?"

"I only had that dream because of all the weird stuff in my head, didn't I?" Trish kicks a stone into the road. "That's what dreams are. Your brain working things out." Which is something else they said on the telly.

But this, it seems, is yet another thing on which she and Kiki don't agree.

"Not always." He shakes his head. "Sometimes dreams are a way of seeing into the future or the past."

"Oh, please…" Trish kicks another stone into the gutter. "We ain't in a film, you know. This is real life. People can't do things like that in real life."

Kiki, however, is not incapable of using logic and reason himself. "All right, so I have a question."

"What?" snaps Trish.

"If you think it's all just a dream and a hologram thingy, why are you telling me about it? Why were you so worked up that you needed to talk to *me*?"

"I'm not *worked up*," says Trish a bit loudly and sourly. "It's only that I want you to come with me to give the picture back to Betty Friedman. I don't want it in my room." But, for some reason, she doesn't feel that she can simply throw it out. "And I don't fancy going on my own."

Kiki doesn't fancy going back to Betty Friedman's under any circumstances – not even with an army or a battery of talismans and spells. Not with that demon lurking about. "I don't know…" He watches his feet fall on the pavement – left, right … left, right … "I don't really want to get involved."

"What do you mean you don't want to get involved?" Trish waves her hands in the air dramatically. "You are involved, in case you didn't know. You're just as involved as I am."

Left, right … left, right … Kiki sighs. "Yeah, I know that. Only—" He decides against mentioning demons just now. "Only I don't want to hurt her feelings. She gave it to us as a present. I mean if she is … you know…"

"A witch?" There is quite a bit of scorn in Trish's voice. "So you reckon that if she is a witch and we give her back the photo she'll get mad and then she'll turn us into pigeons, and then people will poison us or leave out acid so our feet burn off and we die miserable deaths. Is that what you're scared of?"

"Something like that," Kiki mumbles.

"Fine." Trish picks up speed. "If that's the way you want it. If that's all the thanks I get for trying to help *you* out of a bit of bother, then that's just brilliant. You can go home and hide in your cupboard from Betty Friedman and The Wat Boys for the rest of your life for all I care. I'll sort it out myself."

Kiki is torn. Trish is the closest he has come to having a friend and he doesn't want her to be mad at him, but he really doesn't want Betty Friedman to be mad at him either. And he doesn't want to run into her demon. Which is worse? Being turned into a pigeon by Betty Friedman or attacked by the demon, or having Trish tell everyone at school what a baby he is?

As they walk up the main road to the side road that runs back to Wat Tyler House, Fate graciously takes the decision out of Kiki's hands.

Way down at the end he can see The Wat Boys with their bikes, their football gear in bags hung over the handlebars. They're running late today.

"Let's go back down to the shops." Kiki turns round sharply, pulling Trish with him. "I forgot my mum wants me to get some milk. We can talk some more while we do that."

Trish was expecting Kiki to bolt for home, and, since she hasn't spotted The Wat Boys, takes this as a change of heart. "Well?" she prompts as they scuttle back down the hill towards the shops. "Does this mean you'll come with me?"

Because Kiki doesn't want her to abandon him now, not with The Wat Boys on the loose, he gives in. "All right," he says. "But we don't go inside, right? We just hand her the picture at the door and that's it."

"That's fine by me," says Trish. "I don't—" She grabs his arm. "Hang on! We won't even have to go to her door. Look, there she is in front of the video shop."

Betty Friedman is at the zebra crossing, waiting to cross to the other side of the road.

Kiki and Trish start to run.

"Oi! Miss Freedman!" shouts Trish. "Oi! Wait up!"

But Betty Friedman is concentrating on the traffic and doesn't hear her. Satisfied that the road is clear, she steps onto the crossing.

"We can catch her up on—" Trish breaks off as a fancy black car with tinted windows shoots past them like a bullet. The end of her sentence is lost in a scream that is not very different from the way she screamed in her dream.

Trish's scream makes Betty Friedman look up in time to see the car bearing down on her like a cheetah on a gazelle. She jumps back, but this, somehow, is not enough to save her from being hit.

By the time Trish and Kiki reach the video shop

there is already a small crowd gathered round the collapsed form of Betty Friedman.

"Poor old dear," someone is saying. "Shouldn't be out on her own at her age."

"They can't really see, can they?" says a second person.

"Probably has trouble with her feet," says someone else.

Although Trish thinks Betty Friedman is mad as they come, she suddenly finds herself feeling very protective of her. "Of course she can see," snaps Trish. "And she don't have no trouble with her feet, neither. She was *on the zebra*."

The first woman shakes her head. "Poor old dear," she says again.

The newsagent is ringing for an ambulance on his mobile phone and the man from the video shop is telling the old lady that she's going to be just fine.

Trish pushes her way into the circle. "Miss Friedman! Miss Friedman! Are you all right?"

Betty Friedman's eyelids flutter. "Hooshtah... Hooshtah..." she mutters. "There's never a camel when you need one."

She's delirious, thinks Trish. Delirious from the shock.

"Betty!" calls Trish. "Betty! It's me!"

At last Betty Friedman's eyes open. "Trish?"

Displaying the inconsistency of behaviour for which humans are so justly famous, Trish, who only minutes ago wanted nothing to do with Betty Friedman, falls to her knees with relief. Except that her skin is grey and she is lying on the ground, the old woman looks exactly as she did last night. At least she's alive. "Me and Kiki saw the whole thing," says Trish. "We can be witnesses."

"Mrs Calabash…" Betty Friedman's voice seems to come from miles away – slowly and unsurely. "Mrs Calabash can't be left on her own."

"Don't worry," Trish reassures her, "the ambulance will be here soon."

"Never mind the ambulance," gasps Betty Friedman. "Mrs Calabash can't be left on her own. You have to look after her for me." She fumbles in her pocket and pulls out a rusted old key. "Don't leave her by herself. It's very important. You have to promise me that. A solemn promise. Do you understand? Under no circumstances."

Not far in the distance a siren can be heard coming towards them.

Trish, who is possibly in something of a state of shock herself, now completely forgets her fear of re-entering the vicarage – as well as her determination not to do so. All she can think of is the poor cat being left on its own. Trish, of course, is often on her own and doesn't care for it very much. "Sure, I'll look after her." She takes the key from Betty Friedman's hand. "My mum likes cats." Which makes them one of the few things her mother does like.

"And another thing, Trish…" Betty Friedman's voice is fading in rather an alarming way. "Don't forget – you and Kiki must not be afraid to take the initiative. If I'm not there to help you, you must act for yourselves."

"Yeah, right," agrees Trish, who reckons that you don't argue with the delirious any more than the very drunk. "Whatever you say."

The man from the video shop touches Trish's shoulder. "Come on, love. The ambulance is here."

"Don't you worry none, Miss Friedman," says Trish. "I'll take good care of Mrs Calabash."

"Step back, step back…" orders the man from the video shop. Very gently, he pulls Trish to her feet as the doors of the ambulance open and a police car pulls up behind it. "You want to get out of the way, love."

Trish and Kiki step back with the others, and watch as Betty Freedman is carefully moved onto a stretcher.

"Miss Friedman!" Trish calls as they start to

wheel her away. "Miss Friedman, don't worry about the car. We saw exactly what happened."

"And what car would that be?"

Trish looks round to find a policeman standing over her and Kiki.

"What car?" he repeats. "I was told she fell over. Are you saying you saw her get hit by a car?"

Trish nods, only now realizing that the black car is nowhere to be seen.

The policeman takes a notebook from his pocket. "Do you happened to know what sort of car it was?"

Trish shakes her head. "Something really posh."

"It was a Mercedes," says Kiki. His father drives a minicab and is always pointing out the cars he wishes he could afford.

The policeman writes this in his notebook. "I don't suppose you happened to get the number of this Mercedes?"

Trish shakes her head again. It hadn't even occurred to her to look; she'd expected the car to stop.

"I did," says Kiki.

Trish and Kiki Collect Mrs Calabash

No one else on the street at the time of the accident saw the black Mercedes or any other car hit Betty Friedman.

"But you must've seen it," Trish argues with the newsagent. "You said you was looking out the window."

"I saw the old lady fall," says the newsagent, "but I didn't see any car. I'm sure she must have tripped."

The man from the video shop nods in agreements. "Old ladies are always losing their balance, aren't they? If I had a pound for every one I've seen go down in front of my shop, I'd be living in a house in the country."

"You know what the roads are like round here," says the woman who thinks Betty Friedman is a poor old dear. "Might as well be walking on cobbles."

Trish sighs in exasperation. "Crikey, it was big as a boat. How could you all not see it? It practically drove onto the pavement."

"Now, now," murmurs the policeman. "Take it from me, memory is funny. I've never known two witnesses to see the same thing."

"But it was this enormous, posh car," Trish continues to argue. "They *had* to see it."

The policeman puts a hand on her shoulder. "Just calm down, right? You and your friend tell me what you saw, and then I'll take statements from the others."

Trish tells him about seeing the Mercedes practically fly down the road, and Kiki gives him the number from the plates.

The policeman laughs, shaking his head. "I think you two may be letting your imaginations run away with you a bit." He looks down at his notebook. "Seven-seven-five-zero-zero-one-zero-zero-two-two? That's ten numbers you gave me, son, and no letters at all. That can't be right."

For a second Kiki forgets how shy he is. "But that's what it said," he protests. Kiki has an excellent memory.

This time the policeman pats *him* on the shoulder. "We all make mistakes, you know."

Trish can tell that the copper means her and Kiki – not himself or any of the other adults.

I just don't get it," Trish grumbles as they head back to The Wat. "How come no one else saw the Mercedes? It went straight at her. It don't make sense. Were they all struck temporarily blind or something?"

Kiki is so involved in the mysterious car and Betty Friedman's accident that, as they turn into their road, he doesn't even stop to make a charm in case The Wat Boys are still around. "You want to know what I think?"

That's the trouble with being a child, Trish says to herself. Adults don't care what you think. She kicks at an empty crisp bag. "What?"

"I think it was *him*."

"*Him*?"

"You know – that Sir Alistair bloke. I reckon he's some sort of demon."

"A demon?" What with one thing and another it's already been quite a morning, but still Trish has to laugh. She gives Kiki a scathing look. With children like him about it's no wonder adults don't listen to them. "Even if there was such a thing as demons – which there ain't – I really don't think they'd have titles or shake hands with the Prime Minister or drive posh cars, Kiki. They'd live in underground caves on their own and fly or something."

118

"Well what about the number plates, then? I worked out the numbers and if you add them together in threes—"

"You *worked out* the numbers?" interrupts Trish. "What do you mean you worked out the numbers?"

One of the books Kiki has read during his long hours in the library was all about making codes. "Every letter has a corresponding number in the alphabet," he explains. "You know, like A is one. That's the zero-zero-one bit. So when you add up the other two sets they spell SAD. Those are his initials. S-A-D. SAD."

"People don't spell out their names in numbers, Kiki," says Trish. "And even if they did, SAD could stand for anything. Sidney Adam Doolittle... Shirley Anne Davies... Save All Dodos..."

"*Or* it could stand for Sir Alistair Deuce," says Kiki. "Don't you think it's odd that Betty Friedman said he's after her, and then the next day she gets run over by a car with his initials on it?"

"*Maybe* with his initials on it," Trish amends. "And anyway, in this country that's not called evil powers at work. It's called coincidence. You don't really believe that a bloke like him ran over Betty Friedman, do you? You think he got tired of playing golf with all the other lords so he decided he'd

119

mow down an old lady instead?"

"Just because someone has a lot of money and powerful friends doesn't make him a nice person," Kiki argues. "Really bad things are always being done by rich and powerful men. And maybe he didn't do it himself. Maybe he paid someone else to do it for him."

"In *his* fancy car?" It's almost a shame that it has never occurred to Trish to consider a career in law since she obviously has a talent for it. "Why? So nobody would ever connect it to him?"

Outmanoeuvred, Kiki shrugs. "Well *someone* ran her down. And that's what it said on the plates. We saw what we saw."

"I dunno…" Trish may like to dream herself into a different life, but she spends her days in a very real world. "There's always accidents on that road. My mum says they drive down it like they're in the Grand Prix."

"But it came out of nowhere," Kiki reminds her. "One second it wasn't there and the next it was."

"That's what everybody always says when there's an accident," says Trish.

"But this one really did." Overnight Kiki has changed from a boy whose favourite words were "all right" to a boy who can't seem to stop himself from arguing. "Cars just don't materialize out of the air. It has to be—"

"Demons," finishes Trish as they come up to the vicarage.

She starts to go up the crumbled pathway, but Kiki grabs her arm to stop her.

She turns to him with one of her scornful looks. "Now what?"

"It looks different." Kiki's voice, never particularly loud, is almost a whisper.

"What?" Trish, on the other hand, is almost shouting with frustration.

"Shh…" Kiki squeezes her arm. "The house – it looks different."

Trish shakes him off. "It don't look different to me. It looks like it always does. A dump."

"That's what I mean," says Kiki. "It wasn't a dump last night, was it? I remember the door. It was all shiny and black, not like it is now. And look at the windows. They weren't all boarded up like that last night."

Trish's life seems to have become an endless battle between logic and no logic whatsoever. "I don't know. I wasn't really looking. And anyway, it was dark," she says. "And there was a lot happening. You just didn't see it proper, that's all."

"But what about the curtains? Don't you remember? There were curtains in the parlour." Dark blue, velvet drapes.

"Well, that's it, then, isn't it? She put up the

curtains to hide the boards till she got the windows fixed."

"Don't you remember anything? She told us to look out the window. She said if we looked out the window we'd see The Wat Boys. Why would she tell us that if the windows were boarded up?"

Trish doesn't answer, but strides ahead of him, over the rubble to the front door.

"Come on!" she calls. "Let's just get the flippin' cat and go."

Kiki follows very slowly, tapping the roof of his mouth with his tongue and crossing his fingers so hard they hurt. He was hoping that if he lagged behind enough Trish would have opened the door and collected Mrs Calabash before he got there, but she is still standing on the front step with the key in her hand, staring at the door, when he finally reaches her.

"She gave us the wrong blinkin' key, didn't she?" Trish mutters.

The key Trish is holding a long, old, hand-made key with an ornate head.

"No she didn't." Kiki points to the old, hand-made lock low in the door. "It goes in there."

"Um duh…" says Trish. "What about *that* lock, then?" She points to the very new and very modern machine-made lock higher up. "She didn't give me no key for that."

Kiki may later regret not saying, "Yeah, you're right. We might as well go home then," but, for reasons he will never know, it is, of course, not what he says.

"Well, give it a try. Maybe she didn't lock the top." Nonetheless, he takes a cautionary step back as Trish fits the antique key into the antique lock.

The old door creaks slowly open, as though pulled inwards by a ghostly hand. Today the delicate scent of lavender doesn't waft gently towards them; instead the stink of damp and decay hits them head on. Kiki's heart instantly drops to somewhere round his knees and he closes his eyes, but Trish takes hold of his arm and steps bravely over the threshold, pulling him after her.

"Crikey!" she whispers, as the door slams shut behind them.

Curiosity overpowers terror, and Kiki opens his eyes.

The freshly painted woodwork, the newly papered walls, the pristine tiles, the hat rack and the lantern are all gone. The paintwork is yellowed, chipped and peeling, the staircase half-collapsed, the wallpaper (where it hasn't been eaten away by rats or time) faded and scarred with mildew and mould, and the tiles that aren't missing are black with dirt. There are no inner doors, either, just broken frames where they once would have hung – which at least makes it easy to see that Betty Friedman's warm and cluttered parlour has also vanished in an alarming sort of way.

"What'd I tell you?" Kiki's voice makes a whisper sound like a scream.

"What happened?" Trish's head moves back and forth from one side of the hall to the other as she tries to work out where everything's gone.

Kiki knows what happened without having to think about it. What they saw last night was a manifestation – rather like the people and animals he sees all round The Wat – only this one was specially put on for their benefit. Now, however, is not the place or time to explain that to Trish. Kiki is in a Class-A, top-of-the-range state of fear, very similar to the one that gripped him last night when he found himself watching Sir Alistair Deuce on the news. He uncrosses his fingers to reach for the door. "Let's go, Trish. Now."

Trish nods numbly. She may be a logical and practical girl, but that has always been in the ordinary world where you have to watch out for people, not rooms that disappear. At this particular moment in time, Trish is very close to a state of Class-A fear herself. "Right." On the other hand, she is also a stubborn girl and has no intention of giving in to that fear without a fight. "Only first we've got to find the cat."

"Forget the cat," begs Kiki. "Let's just go."

"But we promised Betty Friedman—"

"Forget her, too." This is possibly the first order Kiki has ever given in his life. "Trish, I don't feel safe. We really have to get out of here. Now."

"We'll have to come back later then," says Trish. "To get the cat."

Kiki would gladly promise anything to make Trish leave. "Right," he agrees. "We'll come back later. But now let's just go!"

He pulls at the doorknob.

If he had a more cynical nature, Kiki would probably have been able to predict what would happen next. Or not happen. The door doesn't budge.

"It's locked!" he wails. "We're locked in."

"We can't be." Trish turns the knob, just as Kiki did, and (also just as Kiki did) pulls hard. "It must be the other lock," says Trish. "It's like it bolted itself."

"And we don't have the key," Kiki adds, unhelpfully.

They are still looking at the lock for which they have no key, when they hear voices right outside the door.

"You're certain your chap saw her come out of here?" asks a man with what Trish would describe as a well posh accent.

"Certain as death," says another. "He was in a van across the road."

The second man's voice is remarkable for two things. The first is that his accent is even more well posh than his companion's; the second is that it is a voice both Trish and Kiki have heard before. Since it seems to have been etched into his soul, Kiki recognizes it immediately. He squeezes Trish's arm. "It's *him*," he whispers. "It's Sir Alistair." He starts edging away from the door. Trish, however, stays put, mesmerized by the men's conversation.

"But she couldn't have actually been in the house," says the first speaker. "The place is a death trap. If it was her, she was probably just having a snoop."

"Oh it was her, all right."

"I still don't see…"

"She didn't have the cat with her."

The first man laughs. "So?"

There is no laughter from his companion. "So if she didn't have the cat with her, she left it somewhere. And my guess is that she left it in here. And if she left the cat in here, then perhaps this is where she's hidden the documents as well. If she really does have them, they have to be somewhere. And we know they're not in the church. If you recall, I went through it myself when we first started this."

126

"But you weren't looking for them then."

"No, but I was looking. And I certainly didn't find them, did I?"

"But she can't be staying in this wreck," argues the first man. "Besides, how would she get in? Climb through a broken window?"

"I wouldn't put it past her. But she might not have had to go to such unladylike lengths. She may, of course, have a key."

"She can't have," says the other man with certainty. "I've got the only key."

The second man sighs, very much like someone who's been trying to explain quantum mechanics to a beetroot. "Of course you have. In which case I suggest that you use it. I don't really fancy standing out here all day. This neighbourhood would depress a corpse."

Keys jangle.

"Upstairs!" hisses Trish.

Kiki, who has edged himself to the bottom of the staircase, doesn't need to be told more than once, and, avoiding the broken steps with impressive dexterity, is already crouched behind the balustrade on the first-floor landing by the time Trish joins him.

The front door opens with a painful groan.

The owner of the only key, who is none other than Mr Edward I. Chumbley, the Minister for

Housing, steps inside. "Gordon Bennett!" he exclaims. "What a stink. It's enough to make one gag."

Treading carefully, Sir Alistair Deuce follows him over the threshold. "The stink of history," he replies. "The faster this place is knocked down, the better for the world."

Mr Chumbley peers down the hallway, thickly carpeted with decades of dust and debris. "It looks to me like your man's made some mistake." Mr Chumbley's voice is muffled by the blue silk handkerchief he has produced from his breast pocket and is holding over his mouth and nose.

Sir Alistair extends the look of distaste on his face to include the Minister for Housing. "My man made no mistake."

Sir Alistair sounds very confident. Which, of course, he is. It was Sir Alistair himself who spent the night in the van, crouched in the front seat like a homeless builder. He knew Betty Friedman would come here. It may be a place he loathes, but it is one she loves. She wasn't going to book herself into a hotel when she could be near her precious king – here where the memories of all she held so dear weave in and out through time.

"All right, perhaps not a mistake," concedes Mr Chumbley, "let's call it a misreading. She couldn't have been coming from the house. The last person who stood where we're standing has probably been dead for the past fifty years."

"You think so?" Sir Alistair snorts derisively. "Perhaps it's just as well you never had any aspirations to be a detective, Edward – I can't imagine you would have had any success."

"I take that to mean that I've missed something," says Edward I. Chumbley stiffly.

"Only those fresh footprints going up the stairs."

Mr Chumbley gives a short laugh. "Paw prints. Looks like a cat got in."

"Well of course a cat got in! What have I been trying to tell you?" snaps Sir Alistair. "But, in fact, it isn't the cat that I meant. I meant those – the prints made by shoes."

"They're too small to be the old bag's." Mr Chumbley, who isn't accustomed to being snapped at by members of the aristocracy, is now sounding cold as well as stiff. He looks into the front room. "And there aren't any footprints in there. If you ask me, she hasn't been here at all. The cat's probably just a stray."

"Well, I didn't ask you," says Sir Alistair. "And, although there may be no trace of the ubiquitous and wearisome Elizabeth Martha about, that doesn't mean that she hasn't been here. She'd be careful." Sir Alistair might further explain that

Betty Friedman is too clever a Time Keeper to leave any signs behind, but doesn't. He is very well aware of just how ordinary a man Edward I. Chumbley is. "The question is, who has been here and carelessly left their footprints about?"

"It must be kids," says Mr Chumbley.

"Kids..." repeats Sir Alistair. "By which, I take it, you mean random kids who aren't involved with our friend Miss Friedman." Possibly because he is so devious himself, Sir Alistair's is a suspicious nature. Although he has got the old bag out of the way for the time being, that doesn't mean she hasn't taken precautions. She does, after all, know him well. "And what would children be doing in here?"

"Nothing good. Not the scum round here. It's a miracle they haven't burnt it down by now."

Some of the scum round here peer cautiously around the banister.

"It's interesting, is it not, that the footsteps go up the stairs but don't seem to come back down?" asks Sir Alistair Deuce. "I wonder if our little visitors are still up there, or if they've leapt to their tragic deaths out of a back window and are lying with broken bones and shattered skulls amongst the tins and bottles in the back garden."

Edward I. Chumbley hasn't yet worked out that Sir Alistair Deuce has no sense of humour, and so,

130

assuming him to be joking, laughs – albeit nervously. He eyes the broken staircase uneasily. "You're not suggesting that we go up to look?"

Sir Alistair shakes his head. "No, no I'm not. I have no intention of ruining a two-thousand pound suit and a pair of handmade shoes to find out if some brats are up there or not. Or to find out if our chum, Miss Friedman, has left anything we might like to have hidden under a floorboard. In any event, I have something else to attend to rather urgently myself. I think we can leave the dirty work for my men. I'll have them search the house immediately."

"You might want to put a chap on guard here as well as at the church," suggests Mr Chumbley, trying to repair some of his wounded pride.

"Oh, there's no need for that. She won't be back." He sounds very confident about this, too.

Kiki and Trish are on their feet as soon as the door shuts downstairs.

"Quick," says Kiki, "we've got to get out of here before the house gets searched."

This time it is Trish who doesn't have to be told twice.

They bolt into the nearest room, the one right at the back of the house. Mrs Calabash is curled up on the windowsill. Not a creature easily worried or stressed, she has obviously been asleep, but as

131

Kiki and Trish charge in she opens her eyes and sits up as though she's been patiently waiting for them all along.

"Well, at least we found the cat." Kiki scoops Mrs Calabash into his arms – where she promptly snuggles against him and closes her eyes. He leans to the window, Mrs Calabash purring in his arms, a sound he finds rather reassuring. "What about getting out through here?"

Trish, however, has a very vivid image of their broken bodies lying in the rubble behind the cottage. "Are you mad? We can't climb out the window."

"I think we can." Kiki's years of avoiding The Wat Boys have made him a pretty dab hand at climbing up, over and down high, stationary objects. "It's only one storey, there's a roof right below. We can use the drainpipe to get down to it, and then there's a tree that'll get us to the ground."

"What if the drainpipe don't hold us?" asks Trish.

"What if it does?" counters Kiki.

Trish and Kiki Visit Betty Friedman in Hospital – or Try to

Fortunately for our story, the drainpipe holds fast. Indeed, Trish, Kiki and Mrs Calabash reached the overgrown garden and its rusted tins and broken bottles with so little trouble they might simply have strolled out of the back door – or floated effortlessly to the ground.

"So now what do we do?" asks Kiki.

Trish rolls her eyes. "What do you think? We've got the cat – so now we go home."

One would think that this idea would strike Kiki as a particularly good one – especially as it's one he was arguing for not so long ago – but one, of course, would be mistaken.

"Maybe we shouldn't. Not yet." Although the drop to the ground wasn't a long one, it gave Kiki plenty of time to mull over the events of the last half hour. "If you want to know what I think, I think we should go to the hospital first."

Trish frowns. "Why's that? You ain't hurt, are you?"

Kiki shakes his head. "No, course not. I meant to visit Betty Friedman."

Trish dismisses this suggestion with a sigh. "We can visit her later. Bring her some grapes like they do on the telly." Trish is an energetic girl (and surprisingly healthy for someone who eats as many crisps as she does), but it has been a very tiring morning. "I'm knackered. I need a bit of a lie down before we go traipsing off to the hospital."

Kiki, however, is still shaking his head. "I didn't mean like a social call. I think we need to talk to Betty Friedman. And, you know, make sure she's all right."

"All right?" scoffs Trish. "Course she's all right. She's in hospital, ain't she?"

But Kiki is worried. "Why didn't Sir Alistair come upstairs after us, Trish? You could tell he was suspicious."

"You heard him. He didn't want to mess up his fancy suit and shoes."

"That's not all he said, though." Kiki remembers every word Sir High-and-Mighty spoke. "He said he had something urgent to do himself."

Trish shrugs. "So?"

"So, what if he is suspicious that Betty Friedman's got help? What if he went to make sure she can't talk to us?"

As persuasive as Kiki's argument is, it is not the reason Trish gives in. It is the way Mrs Calabash has sat up and is staring at her with her large, hypnotic eyes.

"Crikey..." mutters Trish. "But you're the one who's ringing up to find what ward she's in."

It was easy enough for Kiki to learn that Betty Friedman is in Jonas Ward. The problem is that Jonas Ward has apparently disappeared.

"This was a really stupid idea," Trish grumbles as they come to a stop at yet another intersection of corridors. She shifts the small bag of apples that she's carrying from one hand to the other. "This place isn't a hospital, it's a blinkin' maze."

"It wasn't a stupid idea," insists Kiki. "I told you. We've got to talk to Betty so we can make sure she's all right and find out what's really going on."

Trish eyes him sourly. "We know what's really going on. We know that Sir Alistair Thingy is after that property – which isn't exactly big news since he is a developer and into progress and all."

"Deuce," says Kiki. "Sir Alistair Deuce. And we know that he tried to kill Betty Friedman. You heard what he said, '*She won't be back*'. So he knows what happened to her."

"Oh, please…" If nothing else, Trish's friendship with Kiki is turning her into an expert on scorn. "If he knows what happened to her why did he come looking for her at the house?"

"Because he wasn't looking for *her*." And Kiki's friendship with Trish is vastly improving his skills of debate. "He was looking for where she'd been. You heard him say that, too – he reckoned she might have hidden the documents in the house."

"But she hasn't," says Trish. "That's another thing we know."

"All right, so we know a couple of things. But we don't know about all the—" He hesitates, searching for a word that won't get him another large dose of Trish's scorn. "You know, about all the strange bits."

He gets another large dose of her scorn just the same. "Crikey, why don't you just say what you mean?" snaps Trish. "You mean the magic stuff." And she widens her eyes and flaps her arms in the air, chanting, "Whoowhoowhoowhoo … whoowhoowhoowhoo…"

"You can make fun all you want," says Kiki, "but you know what I think?"

Trish swings the bag of apples back and forth. "No, Kiki, what do you think?"

Kiki has decided to forget about trying to be diplomatic. When you're dealing with demons and the like it's best to be completely honest. "I think the cottage we were in last night was a manifestation."

There is no flicker of agreement, disagreement or even much interest in Trish O'Leary's eyes. "A manifestation."

"You know," prods Kiki, "a manifestation of the past."

Trish gazes at him as if he may be a manifestation. "What's that meant to mean, then?"

Kiki makes a helpless gesture. "You know... A manifestation of the memories that are – you know, sort of caught in time. So it's almost like a film of the way it was in the past.."

"You mean like those ghosts Betty Friedman says you see?"

So there's nothing wrong with Trish's memory; what a relief.

Kiki nods. "Yeah, something like that. Only I think it's not just that Betty Friedman can travel through time and all, I think she can ... you know, make it do what she wants."

There is a word for this, and Trish knows what it is, since the ex-Mrs O'Leary does it to her on a regular basis.

"Manipulate it," says Trish. "You think she can manipulate time."

"Yeah. That's why everything was gone when we

went there today. Because Betty Friedman wasn't there to bring it all back. Or maybe she erased it on purpose – you know, in case Sir Alistair turned up while she was out, but she left it so we could get in with the key if something happened to her."

"Earth calling Kiki," says Trish. "You're forgetting about coincidence. It was just a coincidence that we was there when she was hit. Like it was a coincidence that she saw us outside the house last night and asked us in."

"I don't think those were coincidences," says Kiki. "I think they happened for a reason."

"No they didn't." Trish sounds very certain. "Things happen, and then, when something else happens, it makes it look like the first thing happened so the second thing could." Trish's mother is a case in point. Trish's mother met Mr O'Leary when she missed her bus and, because she was late (because she couldn't find her keys), was forced to hail a cab. The ex-Mrs O'Leary has always taken this as proof of how Fate has it in for her.

"And you're forgetting about Betty Friedman," points out Kiki.

Trish groans. "Oh, please... You make it sound like she's making it all happen."

Kiki says nothing.

"What you've got to get in your head," Trish steams on, "is that Betty Friedman isn't a witch."

"No, she's a Time Keeper who gave you a key that shouldn't've worked for a house that wasn't really there."

Trish shrugs. "Well…" Next to arguing with Kiki, dealing with the ex-Mrs O'Leary (an irrational woman at even the best of times) is as easy as eating a biscuit.

"There isn't any other explanation and you know it," presses Kiki.

Perhaps not, but Trish dearly wishes that there was.

"No, I don't know it." Trish is not about to give in to Kiki and his superstitions. Not just yet. "What I do know is that we've been walking round for hours and all we do is come back to where we started."

In fact, they have only been walking round the hospital for a little over twenty minutes, but it has been largely in circles and, given how similar the corridors look, does seem much longer.

Trish glances left and right and forwards and backwards, but there are no signs to help them find the ward they're looking for. "I think we should try down there," and she points to the right.

"I don't," says Kiki. "We've already been down there." Probably more than once.

Trish rolls her eyes. "Oh, please… How can you

tell we've already been down there? Every hallway looks the same as every other one."

"I remember that door." Kiki points to a door that looks to Trish just like the door on either side of it, and the doors on either side of them, and all the doors across the way. "See? The handle's got some yellow paint on it. And that light." This time he points to the ceiling to their left. "The bulb's gone."

"Crikey, who are you? Sherlock Holmes?" Trish looks down one corridor and then the other again, hoping for a clue of her own, but they still look no different to all the others they've been in.

Kiki peers down the front of his jacket – two round, golden eyes look back at him. "Mrs Calabash's woken up." He rubs his chin very gently on the top of Mrs Calabash's head, a gesture he believes will bring them luck, which is something they could obviously use. "Maybe that's a sign that we're near Betty Friedman."

"Your signs are about as useful as the hospital's," scoffs Trish. "If she is nearby, then she's made a brilliant recovery and is already walking around, trying to find the way out."

Kiki gazes down the front of his jacket again. "She's starting to hum or something," he reports. "She sounds like a helicopter."

"I told you we shouldn't bring her along.

They'll throw us out if they find we've got a cat with us."

"But she wouldn't let go of me," protests Kiki. "Anyway, it'll cheer up Betty Friedman to see her."

"You mean it will if we ever find Betty Friedman," says Trish.

As if the gods of St Lucy's Hospital have heard her, a nurse suddenly steps through the swinging doors behind them, walking briskly and looking at her watch.

"'Scuse me," says Trish as she passes them.

The nurse stops and turns round. "Are you two on your own?" she wants to know.

Trish isn't certain whether or not children are allowed in the hospital on their own, so she doesn't know what the right answer is. She decides it's better to err on the side of caution. "We're visiting my nan – with my mum," says Trish, who besides being practical is very good at thinking quickly. "Only we went to get some apples and now we can't find Jonas Ward. We've been looking for ages and ages."

"Jonas Ward?" The nurse smiles slightly, nodding at something behind them. "See that door I just came through? The one that says *Jonas Ward*?"

Trish and Kiki both look to the door the nurse just came through. "Oh," they say together.

141

Above the door is a sign that quite clearly says: Jonas Ward.

The nurse laughs. "Let's hope you can find your way out again," she says.

"I don't know how we could've missed that sign," Trish mutters as they open the doors to Jonas Ward.

"We missed it because it wasn't there," says Kiki, "that's how."

"Oh for Pete's sake... Of course it was there." Although Trish knows very well that the sign *wasn't* there, she still says this quite forcibly. "Or do you think Sir High-and-Mighty had it moved as a joke to wind us up?"

Kiki follows her into the ward. "If he did, it wasn't for a joke."

But Trish isn't listening. Having successfully dealt with one nurse, she is already asking the nurse at the reception desk for her dear old grandmother, Betty Friedman.

"Miss Friedman?" The nurse looks at his list. "Here she is. Bed twenty. Oh – that's odd. It says she's been discharged."

"But she can't've been," argues Trish. "We rang up to see where she was only a little while ago. And she only got here this morning. She was pretty banged up."

"I know." He sounds as puzzled as they are. "I

remember them bringing her in. She's quite a character." He squints at the entry. "But that is what it says. Released by Dr..." He looks up at them, grinning. "It's true what they say about doctors' handwriting. It looks like Dr Dunce, but that can't be right. There's no doctor in this hospital named Dunce."

Kiki swallows hard. "Maybe it's not Dunce," he suggests. "Maybe it's Deuce."

The nurse nods. "Yeah, you could be right." He looks up, still puzzled. "But there's no doctor named Deuce in this hospital either."

At last the wall of scepticism, logic, reason and stubborn doubt that has been protecting Trish from Kiki's view of the world – especially as it pertains to them – starts to crumble. She feels, rather than sees, the triumphant look Kiki is giving her.

"No," says Trish. "I don't reckon there is."

What Kiki and Trish Do Next

Kiki looks down at Mrs Calabash – draped over his arms as though she has no bones and sound asleep – as they walk up the side road to the concrete walls of home. "So now what do we do?" he asks.

It is not, of course, Mrs Calabash who answers.

"How should I know?" grumbles Trish. Having to accept that reality is not as straightforward, reliable or one-dimensional as she thought – not even in England – has put Trish in something of a strop. "I'm not the one with magic powers, am I?"

Kiki can feel Mrs Calabash purring against his chest. "I was only asking."

Even Trish's sigh is stroppy. Trish is full of doubts. She can't help wondering what other weird things happen all the time that she doesn't know about. How much of what she believes is an illusion. And for this she blames Kiki. She may have been ignorant before, but at least she was fairly happy. If he wasn't always asking questions, she might, right at this moment, be sitting in front of the telly with a packet of crisps and a smile on her face, instead of trudging up the road with a boy who believes in demons in two-thousand-pound suits. "I reckon we just go home and wait to see what happens," she says. "What else can we do?"

"Well, I was thinking…" Kiki's eyes dart ahead towards St Barnabas. He hugs Mrs Calabash a little tighter, and her purr sounds through his heart. "You know, that maybe we could look for those documents ourselves."

Trish stops so abruptly that Kiki only knows she isn't beside him when he hears her voice behind him squawk, "Look for the documents ourselves? But you heard Sir Alistair. He already searched the church."

Kiki stops as well, turning round, Mrs Calabash gently swinging over his arm like a scarf. "So what?" he asks. "He didn't know where to look, did he? He didn't know about the crypt."

"Have you gone completely mad?" asks Trish.

Kiki can see that this is a distinct possibility. He certainly feels far braver than he usually does; and considerably more reckless. Or perhaps it's simply that recent events, rather than questioning his view of the world, have confirmed it. There's nothing like knowing you're right to increase a person's confidence.

He shrugs. "I only thought that, well, since Sir Alistair's kidnapped Betty Friedman we might be able to use the documents to make him let her go. I mean, that's what he's really after, right? So if we've got the papers there wouldn't be any reason for him to keep her his prisoner, would there?"

"What there would be," answers Trish, "is a really good reason to kidnap us."

Kiki quickly adjusts his thinking to this slight flaw in his plan. "Well what if we took the documents to the Bill?"

"What if we did?" Trish demands. "You think they're going to take our word against the word of Sir Alistair blinkin' Deuce?"

Kiki shrugs again. "But we have to do something, don't we?"

"No, we don't have to do something." Trish sounds extremely clear on this point. Never mind what Betty Friedman said about taking the initiative. It is doing something that has got them in the mess they're in. "We don't have to do nothing. You're the one who says Betty Friedman's got all these magic powers. If she really did make the house appear like that and can make time do what she wants, then getting away from his nibs and finding her blinkin' documents should be easy."

"But maybe it isn't." Kiki can almost feel Mrs Calabash's purr echo through his bones. "And she asked for our help, didn't she? She wouldn't have asked us if it was that simple."

Trish's mouth has become very small and hard. "So?"

"So maybe he wouldn't have caught her if we had."

"You mean you think we owe her something?"

"Well, yeah ... sort of..." Mrs Calabash pushes against him, now sounding as though she's going for lift off. "I don't see why we can't try."

Trish is about to say that if Kiki wants to help Betty Friedman he is welcome to, but he can count her out.

The reason she doesn't say this is because there is the sudden slamming of a door, and a man's voice shouting, "Oi! You two! What're you doin', hangin' round here?"

A large, burly man lumbers towards them from a large blue and yellow van with the words The Futures Development Corporation, Ltd, printed on the side in black and gold. "Oi!" he says again. "You heard me. What're you doing here?" The man acts as if he owns the neighbourhood – or works for the person who does.

It is only now that Trish realizes that she's

stopped right in front of the vicarage. Yet another coincidence one has to assume.

"We ain't doing nothing." Not one to cower before authority, Trish stands very straight, her chin raised. "We live here."

"Not here, you don't." The man gestures to the church and all that surrounds it. "This here's private land. You keep off it."

"It ain't private land, it belongs to the Council," Trish points out. "And anyway, we *are* off it. This pavement ain't private land. And this road ain't neither." She pauses, not sure for a second how to describe what they are, but, as often happens, something she's learned from the telly comes to her aid. "They're public thoroughfares, and that means we've got as much right to stand here as anybody."

The man sighs. "Look, my orders are to keep everyone away from here." Especially children. His orders are very clear on that. "So why don't you just do as you're told and go home?"

Mrs Calabash opens her eyes, leaning heavily against Kiki's chest. Which seems to have the effect of making him feel braver still. "And if we don't?" he wants to know.

"Yeah," says Trish, "what're you going to do? Beat up little kids?"

They man heaves another sigh. He has no intention, of course, of beating up little kids. On the other hand, if he doesn't keep them away from the church he could lose his job. His orders are very clear on that point as well. "I'll call the police, that's what I'll do. You can be done for being a nuisance, you know."

But the telly has also taught Trish quite a bit about the law. "And you could be done for wasting police time," she counters.

The man, however, knows that an employee of Sir Alistair Deuce's is unlikely to be arrested for anything short of murder. "You think so, Little Miss Know-it-all?" He pulls his phone from his pocket and shakes it at them. "I'm promising you, if you don't leave I'm ringing the Bill."

What child, given the choice between being hauled in by the constabulary and backing off, would continue to argue?

Not Kiki. It would break his parents' hearts if he ended up in jail. "Come on," he says, tugging Trish's arm. "Let's go home."

Trish, however, is precisely the sort of child who stubbornly refuses to back down. "Go on," she says. "Call the coppers. See if we care!"

"Right." Sir Alistair's man bends his head and jabs his finger at the buttons on his phone.

As coaches are always advising their players, it is never a good idea to take your eyes off the ball.

Which is precisely what the security guard has done. As if she somehow knows this, Mrs Calabash suddenly leaps from Kiki's arms, and (in what can only be considered a well-concealed ability to move very quickly) races from the public thoroughfare and into the grounds of the church.

"Oh, no!" moans Trish. "The cat's got away!"

"Mrs Calabash!" screams Kiki.

Sir Alistair's man looks up to see Trish and Kiki running after her.

"Oi!" he bellows. "What'd I tell you?"

"Our cat!" gasps Kiki. "We have to get our cat."

Whatever distinctions there were between private property and public thoroughfares before have sped away with Mrs Calabash. Now there is no doubt whose land Trish and Kiki are on, which makes it easy for the guard to know what to do next. He gives chase.

"Come back here you two!" he shouts. "I told you to stay out of there!"

In answer, Mrs Calabash, Trish and Kiki all pick up speed, scrabbling over the debris of the churchyard in a way that the guard, who has eaten a few more portions of chips and drunk a few more beers than are strictly good for him, can't hope to match.

Mrs Calabash scoots towards the side of St

Barnabas, and Trish and Kiki follow, reaching the outside entrance that leads to the crypt. Boards have been nailed across the heavy door, but not, as luck and coincidence would have it, across the hole at the bottom. The silver tabby slips through.

"Now what?" asks Kiki.

"Come back here!" the guard is half-shouting, half-panting. "You're for it now!"

Trish watches Mrs Calabash's tail flick as though beckoning them on, and then disappear. It is not a large hole, but neither of them is a large child. "We go after her, don't we?" says Trish, who seems to have forgotten that she was against the idea of going into the church. Before Kiki, who seems to have forgotten that he was for it, can suggest an alternative action, she throws herself on the ground and wriggles through. Kiki dives after her.

"It's like she knows where she's going," whispers Trish as they get to their feet.

"She probably does," he whispers back.

They can hear Mrs Calabash scampering down the stairs to the crypt, but it is too dark to see her – or anything else for that matter.

"Now we've lost her," whispers Kiki. "I can't even see my feet."

"Hang on." Trish pulls her keys out of her pocket and snaps on the tiny torch.

Now Kiki can see his feet. Though not much more. Very cautiously, they descend the narrow, worn down steps.

Outside, the guard has finally caught up with them and is pounding on the door. "Out!" he gasps. "Get out of there now!"

"Come on." Trish grabs Kiki's hand as they reach the greater darkness of the crypt itself. "I think I can hear her." She can only hope that what she hears isn't a rat.

Following the motor-like sound being made by Mrs Calabash more than the feeble beam of light, they carefully make their way across the dank, damp chamber, trying not to touch any of the mould-covered tombs as they pass. Considering the size of the church, it is a remarkably long journey.

Mrs Calabash is scratching at a stone that lies flat on the ground. Although it looks as though it must mark a grave, there are no dates carved on it, no name and no sad words of loss or love. Mrs Calabash turns her head to look at Kiki her eyes large and gold and far brighter than Trish's tiny torch.

Kiki turns to Trish. "I think she's trying to tell us something, I reckon the trapdoor to the old crypt's under there."

"Brilliant," says Trish. "So now all we need's a

couple of weightlifters to get it up."

"Maybe not." Surely Betty Friedman would have thought of that. Kiki squats down beside Mrs Calabash and takes hold of the stone. It is as easy to lift as a sheet of paper. The trapdoor has rotted, but the stairs that lay beneath it, though crumbling, are still there. Mrs Calabash dashes down them, her eyes now so much brighter than the torch that they have no trouble following her. And no trouble seeing the two large stone sarcophagi in the centre of this second chamber and, beneath a carpet of debris and vegetation, the rows of headstones set into the dirt floor.

"This must be the crypt Betty Friedman was on about," says Kiki.

"So the kid should be round here somewhere." Not sure of which way is east or which west, Trish looks to their right, and Mrs Calabash helpfully turns her head in that direction, too, so they can see the crumbling walls streaked with damp.

"There!" cries Kiki, who does have a sense of direction. "There's the niche. Right where she said."

And in the niche, black and green with moss and mould, is a small but elaborately carved stone sarcophagus. The body of the sarcophagus is covered with obscure symbols and dozens of stars, and on the lid is a sleeping infant, its tiny hands

153

crossed on its chest like wings.

But this moment of happy triumph is fleeting – as moments of happy triumph often are. Trish and Kiki exchange a look that is far from triumphant and even further from happy. Despite Betty Friedman's assurance that the shroud is intact, neither of them particularly wants to be the one to open the sarcophagus to find out if the documents are in it or not.

"I reckon we should both do it." Living with the ex-Mrs O'Leary has given Trish a talent for compromise. "You know, together."

Kiki nods. "That's fair." Together is very often easier than alone.

Hand in hand, they slowly approach the niche.

"On the count of three," whispers Trish, holding her torch ready in her left hand. "One ... two ... three..."

They both catch their breath as they lift the lid and peer in. As Betty Friedman promised, the shroud covering the child's body is still intact – and still white as a winter moon – but there is nothing else with it in the coffin.

"Well," says Kiki. "I guess that clobbers that idea."

As if in answer, Mrs Calabash gives a rather unsettling howl, and jumps from the step where she has been patiently waiting and onto a moss-covered headstone nearby – instantly vanishing from sight.

"Maybe not," says Trish, and she grabs Kiki's hand and leaps onto the headstone, too.

Which they pass through as effortlessly as two of Kiki's ghosts might – or as effortlessly as Mrs Calabash did.

Meanwhile, outside the boarded door to the crypt, the still-panting guard bends down and picks up a small rectangle of paper from the ground. It is a photograph of St Barnabas taken nearly one hundred and fifty years ago. The photograph, of course, fell from Trish's pocket as she squirmed into the church. The guard slips it into his own pocket, hoping that it's important enough to save him his job.

Now Look What You've Done!

Feeling slightly shaken (which is, of course, to be expected), Trish blinks several times and peers around her. She can tell from the feel of grass beneath her hands that they are no longer in the crypt, but it is so deeply silent (no sound of planes, or helicopters, or sirens, or cars, or even voices) that they could very well be under it. The torch is still in her hand, and she shines its light in front of her. "Cor..." Trish's voice is no more than a breath. They are in a dark, unlighted night, curtained with a thick and shifting fog; in a world not of substance but of shadows – tree shadows ... fence shadows ... the shadows of broken walls. It is as if they have fallen through the crypt and straight into a horror film. She turns to her companion. "Now look what you've done!" she hisses.

Kiki has kept his eyes shut while he makes certain that he is still in one, unbroken, piece and that his fingers and toes (so necessary for making charms) are all in good working order, but he opens them now. "What do you mean, look what *I've* done? Look what *you've* done! You're the one who jumped on that headstone."

"And you're the one who got us into this whole mess in the first place," counters Trish.

They might have continued this exchange for some time, but Kiki finally becomes aware of what is around them – which, of course, is not very much and rather unsettling.

"Trish?" he whispers. "Trish, do you think we're dead?" He doesn't feel dead, but, judging by his grandmother's stories, he isn't certain that he would necessarily know. The deep shadows and deeper silence that surrounds them doesn't really make it look like they're still in the land of the living.

Hearing the fear in Kiki's voice does wonders for Trish's own wobbly morale. Her usual pluckiness returns, elbowing aside all thoughts of having landed in a horror film. "Course we ain't dead." She, at least, feels certain she would be able to tell.

"Then what happened?" demands Kiki. Mrs Calabash, who, having expended a great deal of energy in a very short period of time, is asleep on his lap, begins to purr.

"How should I know? Maybe there wasn't nothing under that stone and we fell through some sort of hole or something."

"And came out where?" asks Kiki. "In China?"

"I didn't say for definite," snaps Trish. "I said or *something*."

"You know what I think?" Kiki strokes the sleeping cat.

"No." Trish sighs. "What do *you* think?"

"I think we went through the Portal."

Which may, or may not, be better than being dead.

"You and your blinkin' Portals." Trish sighs again. "I know a lot of weird things have been happening, Kiki, but even you can't believe that you can travel through time just by jumping on a grave. I mean, it wasn't exactly a major cosmic experience, was it? We was in the crypt, and now we're here." Indeed, it was very like the time she borrowed Davey Blyther's skateboard and went straight into a wall – a flash of light, one second of absolutely nothing and then she woke up on the ground.

Kiki would be the first to admit that if they did go through the Portal it was nothing like he thought it would be. He'd imagined that going through a Time Portal would be like entering a kaleidoscope of ghosts tumbling through a tunnel of white light amidst whirlpools of stars – not a we-were-there-and-now-we're-here black gap.

"Then how did we get *here*?"

"I told you." Trish stands up. "We fell through a hole."

Kiki scoops Mrs Calabash into his arms and also gets to his feet, peering into the pervading if shifting gloom. "Then how come we're *outside* and in a graveyard?"

"A graveyard?" Trish focuses on the shadows of broken walls in front of them, finally realizing that they are actually headstones. She turns round to see what's behind them. Only a few metres away is St Barnabas. Trish laughs with a certain amount of relief. Not only are they not in a horror film, but they haven't been thrown into some netherworld beneath the crypt either. She looks over at Kiki. "See? What'd I tell you? We fell through a hole and into the graveyard."

Kiki is far from convinced. "We fell *down* and went *up*?

"Why not?" demands Trish. "We've been in a house that don't exist, what's the difference? And anyways, we're here ain't we? Pretty much right where we started. I recognize those gargoyles at the windows."

"They have ears," says Kiki.

"So?"

"So I never saw them with ears before." Kiki hugs Mrs Calabash close. "Which, if you want to know what I think, means that we went back in time."

"Yeah, but…"

"Yeah but what?" demands Kiki.

The beam of Trish's torch flits through the darkness like a luminous moth, moving in a close circle around them. From what can be seen, the walls of the church are solid and clean, the gargoyles and windows all intact. The grass is cut and not overgrown with weeds. The headstones stand like soldiers on parade, not toppled together like soldiers who have been shot. She can even make out the wrought iron fence that surrounds the churchyard through a gap in the fog. This is not the St Barnabas across from The Wat; this is the St Barnabas of Betty Friedman's photograph – the St Barnabas of Trish's dream.

"Yeah, but it's well dark, ain't it?" says Trish. "We can't really be sure where we are – or when – till morning."

Kiki's stomach rumbles with hunger and he shivers from the chill of the night. "So what do you think we should do now?"

"Not much." The beam of Trish's torch sweeps round where the road and the car park and the tower blocks will one day be, but now there is

160

only darkness and fog. "There's no point in leaving here till daylight, is there? I mean, it's not like we have anywhere to go."

This answer, containing as it does no mention of food or shelter, is not what Kiki was hoping Trish would say. "But shouldn't we find something to eat?"

"Find something where? We're in a graveyard. And we can hardly see more than a couple of centimetres in front of us." Trish pulls half a bar of chocolate from her pocket that looks as though it may have been there quite a while. "I've got this. It'll have to do us till tomorrow."

"But we can't just stay out here all night." Kiki is starting to sound a bit tetchy. "Mrs Calabash doesn't have a jacket, like we do. She'll catch cold."

Kiki isn't the only one getting tetchy. "Crikey! How am I supposed to know the answers to all your stupid questions? It's not like any of this was my idea, is it?" To think that all this has happened because she was trying to help him out. Next time she'll mind her own business. Assuming, of course, that there is a next time for anything. "If it was, I would've made sure we had some sarnies, a couple of blankets and a coat for the blinkin' cat with us, wouldn't I?"

"I only meant—"

"And anyway," Trish steams on, "I'm not the big expert on all this *whoowhoowhoo* stuff. That's *you*. You're the one's meant to know what happened and what we should do."

"I think that's a bit harsh," says Kiki. "I mean, it's not like it was my idea, either. And I never said I was an expert. All I said was—"

"All right, all right." Trish has no desire to spend the night in a graveyard in the fog arguing with Kiki. "What about St Barnabas?" She trains the beam of her torch on the entrance at the side of the church – which now has no boards across it – and walks towards it. "Maybe we can get inside."

"No one's going to leave it un—" Kiki's pessimistic prophecy is cut short by Trish opening the door.

She looks back at him. "You see?" Trish finally has something to smile about. But the smile vanishes immediately. Beyond the church's boundaries, the fog suddenly thins, allowing her to see the shadow moving quickly towards them. And experiencing one of those moments that rarely occur even to the most intuitive and cosmically attuned – and never to the sort of person Trish has always thought herself to be – she knows precisely what is going to happen next; she has seen it before. "Quick!" she hisses. "Hide!" And she drops behind the shrub by the door, pulling Kiki down beside her.

Mrs Calabash stops purring and sits up so that her head is next to Kiki's as he crouches on the ground. Every hair on her body is standing on end, inflating her to twice her normal size, and her eyes are open to golden slits that somehow seem to light the dark and cut through the fog.

But neither Trish nor Kiki is paying any attention to Mrs Calabash or her size. They are watching a girl in a blue dress hurrying over the dirt road that runs between the churchyard and the green, a large bundle wrapped in a shawl held tightly in her arms. Now they can hear the girl's footsteps – urgent as fear – and behind them a heavier, determined tread and, behind those, still well in the distance, hoof beats. The girl puts her hand to the wrought iron gate at the front of the church as the shadows shift around her. And, just as he did in Trish's dream, a man in a coat and hat so black he almost melts into the night suddenly materializes behind the young woman in blue. Trish opens her mouth to shout out a warning but suddenly remembers about not interfering and shuts it again. The man grabs the girl round the waist and clamps a handkerchief over her mouth. One hand still on the gate of the church, the girl collapses against him, and he starts to drag her towards the carriage that has stopped nearby.

"Get down here and give me a hand!" the man bellows.

The boy driving the carriage, who is no older than Kiki and Trish, obediently jumps to the ground.

Hardly daring to breathe, Kiki and Trish watch the man and the boy bundle the girl into the carriage and drive off.

No one moves or speaks for a few minutes after the night falls dark and still once more.

It is Kiki who turns to Trish. "Coo..." he breathes. "It was just like your dream. Didn't I tell you we went through a Portal?"

Trish continues to stare at the spot where the girl in the blue dress was carried away. Trish has been forced to accept quite a few things as real that not twenty-four hours ago she would have said were nothing more than fantasy or science fiction. But to accept that she has just watched the re-enactment of her dream means not only that they have indeed gone through a Portal, but that at least one of time's memories has somehow found its way into her mind.

Kiki gives her a nudge. "So you believe me now, right? You saw the carriage, Trish. There aren't any horses and carriages any more, not in London. Or people dressed like that."

In answer, Trish gets back on her feet and runs to the open gate in front of the church. She bends down for a second and then straightens up, pulling it shut and stuffing something into the pocket of her jeans.

"What's that?" asks Kiki as Trish rejoins him.

"The girl dropped a glove."

"A glove?" Kiki could understand if it was a packet of biscuits, but a glove doesn't seem like the most useful thing that they might acquire right now. "What do you want that for?"

"Dunno." Trish marches past him, stuffing the glove into her pocket. "Come on," she orders. "Let's get inside before something else happens."

A Lucky (or Coincidental) Encounter

Despite the fact that they slept fitfully on hard wooden pews with only fear as a pillow, it is already late morning when Kiki and Trish open the side door of the church the next day.

The sun, all on its own in an empty sky, shines down on an unfamiliar, almost rural landscape. St Barnabas sits at the head of a large green, but the cottages that once clustered round it are gone and the terraces (and, eventually, tower blocks) that will replace them are yet to be built. Past the far side of the green lies the canal, its towpath open and unpaved, but though grand, stuccoed houses can be made out on the hills in the distance, the elegant arc of villas that line its opposite side in the twenty-first century have also yet to be built. Beyond the vicarage, the main road with its shops that Trish and Kiki know so well is no more than a dirt track through undeveloped fields. The only recognizable thing is the church itself, towering over a world where high-rises, satellite dishes and aeroplanes are still to be imagined.

Mrs Calabash, who always sleeps well, dashes out between their legs, Trish and Kiki following her more cautiously.

"Crikey," says Trish. "If it wasn't for St Barnabas, you wouldn't know where you was."

Kiki nods. "It's like it's been moved to a different planet."

And them with it, of course.

Kiki gazes towards the green, seeing again the shadowy fog of the night before. St Barnabas being as full of ghosts as ever, it took him a very long time to fall into even the lightest sleep. To keep his mind off the ghosts, Kiki went over all the things that had happened to him and Trish in the last two days. Betty Friedman rescuing them from The Wat Boys … their witnessing of the accident … Mrs Calabash running away from them … squeezing through the small hole in the door … falling through time … the girl in the blue dress… The more he thought about these things, the more obvious it seemed to Kiki that they weren't simply a collection of random incidents (or coincidences, as Trish would say). It was more like one of those join-the-dot puzzles that little kids do. If he connected the things that had happened to him and

Trish they started to make a picture. He wasn't certain what the picture was yet, but it definitely had a shape and a form. Everything that had happened had brought them here – and not by accident. They were meant to help Betty Friedman. They were meant to find the Portal. They are meant to be here in this particular time and place.

"You know what I think?" he says, but for once doesn't give Trish the opportunity to say no. "I think we should find that bloke from last night. I mean it makes sense, doesn't it? Him and the girl are part of this, or you would never have got that dream in your head. That means he's one of the reasons we're here."

"And how do you reckon we find him?" asks Trish. "We don't even know who he is."

Which, of course, is a valid point – and one Kiki can't actually answer.

"Anyway, if you want to know what *I* think for a change," Trish goes on, "I think we should get something to eat and drink before we do anything else." She gives him one of her more scornful looks. "Unless you ain't hungry any more."

"No, of course I—"

"Right," says Trish. "So first we get some food, and then we can talk about everything and work out what to do next."

Having been reminded of his hunger, Kiki is only too happy to agree. "All right. I reckon that's a good idea." Soldiers, after all, are not the only people who travel on their stomachs. He looks around them as though hoping to discover that a McDonald's has suddenly appeared on the green. "But there aren't any shops or cafes."

"We don't need no shop or cafe." Trish's eyes are on the house once so memorably occupied by Betty Friedman. "We can ask the vicar. He's paid to be good, ain't he? He'll help us out." And she immediately marches down the neat stone pathway that cuts through the churchyard, Kiki hurrying after her. Mrs Calabash, however, stays where she is, stretched out in the grass, staring into the distance, her tail thumping rhythmically against the ground.

The house is quiet, the blue velvet drapes at the parlour window drawn. Nonetheless, Trish (who is unused to either vicars or asking for favours) knocks on the door in an extremely polite manner. There is no answer. She knocks again, a little louder this time, but still she hears no footsteps hurrying towards the door.

The drapes aren't pulled completely closed, and Trish peers in the window through the narrow opening. "I can't see much, but it don't look like anyone's there," she reports.

Kiki glances up at the sun, whose movements he still knows how to read. "It must be getting on to lunch time," he says. "Maybe they're round the back in the kitchen."

"I don't think so." Trish squints hard through the gap. "It looks like everything's covered in sheets."

Discouraged and not a little disheartened at this unsatisfactory end to Trish's good idea, they follow the front path to the stone pavement that runs alongside the wrought iron fence.

"So what do you reckon?" asks Kiki. "You think we should look for a shop or stay round here in case something happens?"

Trish is about to say that the only thing that will happen if they stay here is that they'll faint from hunger, but, before she can, her attention is caught by the notice board at the entrance gate. "Oi, look at this," she says. "What'd I tell you? He ain't here."

Kiki stops beside her. "Who's not here?"

"The vicar." Trish reads out the sign that has been tacked to the board. "'Whilst the roof of St Barnabas is being repaired thanks to the generosity of Dr Erasmus Prole, Christian and Patron of this parish, the Reverend James A. Shillibeer will be on extended leave and services will be held in St Mary's in the Field till further notice.'" She gives

170

him a big smile. "So all we have to do is find this other church and ask the vicar there for help. It can't be too far." And it should be easy enough to see the spire since there's nothing blocking the view. "Where's Mrs Calabash?"

Kiki looks through the bars of the fence to the spot where Mrs Calabash was last seen sunning herself. She isn't there.

"Mrs Calabash!" Kiki stands on tiptoe on the stone foundation to get a better view of the cemetery. "Mrs Calabash! It's time to go!"

But Mrs Calabash, of course, has already gone.

"There she is!" cries Trish. "Over by the canal."

Mrs Calabash, who is indeed hurrying along the canal as though she's going to be late for an important meeting, stops suddenly and looks round. Her tail moves back and forth rather slowly and very deliberately. Her golden eyes glow.

"Wait there!" shouts Trish.

But obedience is not among Mrs Calabash's outstanding qualities. With one last flick of her tail, she turns and rushes ahead.

"She wants us to follow her," translates Kiki.

"It's well lucky you can speak cat, ain't it?" says Trish, but despite her sarcasm she follows Kiki's lead and breaks into a run.

Once they are behind her, Mrs Calabash slows

her pace to a leisurely stroll. She takes the long, scenic route, stopping now and then to sniff at the ground or roll in the grass or scratch at a tree. Dark clouds move in from the east, obscuring the sun, but Mrs Calabash continues to follow the canal until it reaches the southern border of a very exclusive neighbourhood of mansions and villas. It is now that Mrs Calabash suddenly leaves the path, crosses the broad, tree-lined avenue that bridges the canal, and comes to a stop at the corner.

"Oh, brilliant," grumbles Trish, as she watches Mrs Calabash start to groom herself fastidiously. "Follow the blinkin' cat." Her tone and look have reached a new level of scorn. "Follow the blinkin' cat to where? To nowhere, that's where." There are no shops or cafes here – and no sinister men in dark cloaks and hats either. "I don't know why I listen to you." Trish leans against the high wall of the end house, feeling weak with disappointment as well as hunger. "I really don't. I must be mad, too."

Kiki is just as bewildered as Trish by this new development, but he is not yet ready to give into her hunger-fuelled gloom. "Maybe she's just resting," he says. "You have to have faith."

"I'm not interested in faith," snaps Trish. "I just want a sandwich and a cup of tea."

"You'll see," Kiki promises. "Mrs Calabash wouldn't stop for no reason. Something's going to happen."

"Yeah, right," mutters Trish, "we're going to starve to death." Trish sits down on the ground so that when that moment comes she won't have far to fall.

But on this occasion, Trish's pessimism is unfounded. Something is about to happen. The unlikely cause of this *something* is Mrs Prudentia Stump who, even as Kiki and Trish slump together against the wall, is bearing down on them like Fate itself (in another of Trish's coincidences or Kiki's purposeful dots, depending on which view you agree with).

As it happens, Mrs Stump, a thin woman whose sharp features look as though they were chiselled out of stone rather than grown from living cells, is the housekeeper of the generous (and extraordinarily wealthy), Christian and Patron of the parish of St Barnabas – Dr Erasmus Prole.

Mrs Stump is in what she herself would describe as an agitated state, muttering under her breath and walking far more quickly than is usual for a woman of her age and station. Mrs Stump, like Kiki and Trish, isn't in the best of moods. It has been a day of distressingly hard work and considerable emotional pressure (which is not the way

173

Mrs Stump likes her days to be). The day has been one of distressingly hard work because last night the girl went mad and the boy was run over. Regrettably, due to Dr Prole's eccentricities and demanding nature, losing help is not that unusual an occurrence in Mrs Stump's life, but it is unusual for them to go mad, die, or both leave at the same time, and the fact that these three things happened on the very same day meant, of course, that everything fell on her bony shoulders. The day has also been one of considerable emotional pressure because Dr Prole himself has been in a mood as black as the bottom of a coal pit since yesterday. Dr Prole is a singularly difficult and impatient man, even when his mood is diamond bright, but when Dr Prole isn't happy his needs and standards shoot up to impossible heights and his impatience knows no bounds. All morning long it's been "Mrs Stump!" this and "Mrs Stump!" that, with a great deal of banging doors and stomping in and out. That is why now, at an hour when she would very much like to be sitting in front of the fire with a cup of tea and a slice or two of cake, the much-put-upon Mrs Stump is hurrying to get to the servants' registry office before it closes because under no circumstances can she be expected to endure another day like this – not with her weak heart and her sensitive nature.

Mrs Stump has only just reached the road where she hopes to find a cab when she sees two young boys lolling against a mansion wall in the way that young boys, in Mrs Stump's experience (and to her great displeasure), often do. One might expect the unusual dress of these boys to make Mrs Stump (who has some high standards of her own) recoil in horror, but in fact she barely notices. Not only does she have enough on her mind already, but when you work for someone like Dr Prole (who not only travels all over the world but has brought some rather peculiar bits of it back with him) you aren't bothered by little oddities of dress. No, what Mrs Stump is thinking as she approaches the children is that they are the right age for her needs and look bright enough to do what's required but not bright enough to cause any trouble, which, really, is all she asks. It is a pity that one of them isn't a girl. Mrs Stump is in some ways a very stupid woman, but not in all ways. She knows that if she finds employees without the help of the registry office, she won't have to pay a fee and can therefore put that money in her own pocket. As an added bonus, since these two are obviously foreign, they may be presumed to be both desperate for work and unaware of the going rates for domestic help, which would add another few pounds to her savings. As there is no longer a Mr

Stump, Mrs Stump has to look to her future for herself.

As Mrs Stump reaches the corner, the smaller of the two boys says, "I don't know why you're mad at me, Trish."

As Trish is not a name normally given to a boy, Mrs Stump takes a few steps back from the kerb and turns to give them a closer look. It is true. Though wearing trousers and with hair no longer than the bottom of his ear, the larger of the boys is definitely a girl. An ungainly and unattractive one, perhaps, but definitely a girl.

"Pardon me." Mrs Stump is not a woman who smiles very frequently, but she makes the effort, forcing the sides of her mouth into the shape of a very shallow boat. "Is it possible that the two of you are looking for employment?"

"Employment?" repeat Trish and Kiki.

"Yes, employment. You have to earn your bread like the rest of us, don't you?" She nods, and the shallow little boat bobs. "My name is Mrs Stump, and as it happens, I am looking for a girl as a maid-of-all-work and a boy for the house and the stable and whatnot. Room and board and—" Mrs Stump hesitates, judging how low she can make their wages to increase her own profit "three pound a year for each of you."

Finished with her ablutions, Mrs Calabash has

nestled herself under Kiki's jacket and now, pressing against his body as though she is part of his shirt, begins to purr in the way she has that is so reminiscent of a helicopter hovering overhead, the sound echoing through Kiki's bones. He glances down into his jacket. Two large, golden eyes are staring back at him in a very purposeful way. To the surprise of Mrs Stump, who was expecting to have to go up to four pounds at the very least, and of Trish, who was about to turn down the house-keeper's so generous offer without a second thought, Kiki says, "You've got a deal."

Kiki and Trish Are Welcomed into the World of Child Labour

Freed from a journey to the servants' registry office (and freed from having to carry her own shopping), Mrs Stump has done the errands that all the turmoil of the morning kept her from, and now leads the way to Dr Prole's, one hand holding her umbrella high and the other attempting to keep her skirts from the muddy streets, which are strewn with an astonishing array of garbage, dung and small animal corpses flattened by the unruly traffic – that makes the empty crisp packets and drinks cans of the twenty-first century seem like rose petals in comparison. Mrs Stump isn't precisely sailing along – there are still too many people and livestock about for that – but she does walk quite briskly. Trish and Kiki, who couldn't hold an umbrella even if they had one, struggle to keep up with her, burdened as they are by Mrs Stump's purchases. Mrs Calabash, unhappy about being squashed by those purchases, walks between them for shelter from the rain, but otherwise seems at home and unfazed by the turbulence of the streets.

While she walks, Mrs Stump begins to talk about her (and, therefore, their) benevolent employer, Dr Erasmus Prole.

Remembering the sign on St Barnabas' notice board, Kiki gives Trish a look. His faith in Mrs Calabash was obviously well-placed after all.

"Dr Prole?" says Trish, ignoring Kiki's satisfied look. "We've heard of him."

"Of course you have," says Mrs Stump. "Everyone's heard of Dr Prole. He's a gentleman like no other. I bless the day he offered me a place with him. And so should you." Rain drips from her umbrella onto the heads of Trish and Kiki and the spray from passing carriages and carts covers their feet. "Of course he does have a temper – as great men do, they say. Quite a temper. Biblical, if you knows what I mean. Got his dander right up last night, he did." She lifts her skirts a bit higher and launches herself into the mucky road. "Came back unexpected, didn't he? Said he'd be going straight on to dinner from the hospital, but he forgot something or other and came home instead. First I knew was when he opened the front door and cried out, 'What's that creature doing here?'

First I knew there was a cat in the house, either. My instructions are *never* to let no animals in the house because of all his knick-knackery and antiquities, and I never have. True to nature, I dropped everything to rush upstairs to see to the cat, but by the time I got there it was dead as Judas. Got its neck broken in the door. Dr Prole didn't say a word, just marched off to his study, leaving me to get rid of the carcass. I didn't know the girl had already run off, did I? I was still shouting for her to help with the cat when he came tearing out of his study like a runaway horse, and straight back into the carriage what was waiting for him at the kerb. And all without a word to *me*. I never saw the likes in all my days."

Dr Erasmus Pole is, as Mrs Stump explains in great and increasingly tedious detail, one of the most prominent and influential citizens not merely of London but of the entire Empire. But it is only now, as Mrs Stump turns into a graceful square of stuccoed villas, that Kiki and Trish begin to realize that they are farther from The Wat than a mere century or two.

"Dr Prole built this square himself." Mrs Stump makes it sounds as though, beside his many other talents, Dr Prole is a skilled bricklayer, but what she means of course is that amongst Dr Prole's many other talents he is a shrewd property speculator and developer.

"Cor…" whispers Kiki. "This is well posh."

"Stinking rich," whispers Trish.

Mrs Stump stops at Number 33, the largest and grandest of these large, grand houses. Ornate Greek columns hold up the central portico, and life-sized statues stand outside the top floor as though on guard. "Hurry up, you two!" She steps through the gate and starts to descend the cellar stairs. "You're not being paid to dawdle, you know!"

By the time Kiki and Trish catch up with her, Mrs Stump has opened the outer door to the basement, and is standing in the space between the coal cellar and the house, lighting a candle in a brass holder, her umbrella propped against the wall.

"Mind you wipe your feet," she warns as the inner door swings open. "This may only be the servants' entrance but it's still part of Dr Prole's house and you'll treat it accordingly."

Distracted by the ostentatious opulence of Dr Prole's residence, Trish and Kiki have forgotten about Mrs Calabash temporarily, but Mrs Calabash has not forgotten about them. She has followed them down the cellar stairs and softly pads behind them as they follow Mrs Stump inside. Nevertheless, perhaps because she has heard what Mrs Stump has to say about animals, Mrs Calabash stops just inside the door, melting into the dark of the corner – where she closes her eyes and becomes virtually invisible.

Holding the candle before them, Mrs Stump leads the way down the narrow hall to the vast kitchen at the back.

It is a cavernous room, with a scullery and a pantry off it, furnished with a multitude of counters, cupboards, shelves and drawers, a large wooden table, a sink, a range and an oversized hearth in which embers still glow, though not enough to disguise the dank and chill.

Mrs Stump lights a lamp on the table, stokes the fire and, without inviting Trish and Kiki to do the same, removes her cloak and hangs it on a hook by the garden door. These small tasks done, she sits herself down in a chair near the struggling fire and turns to her new employees, who are still standing in the doorway, unsure of what they are meant to do next. Mrs Stump, who prides herself on her Christian kindness, tells them, "Don't just stand there like statues. Put those parcels on the table and step over here where I can have a proper look at you."

The half-hearted fire in the hearth and the flickering lamp throw very small and unenthusiastic circles of light over the table and Mrs Stump, making both her and the kitchen look about as cheerful and inviting as a mortuary. Trish and Kiki's only move is to step closer together.

"Are you deaf?" bawls Mrs Stump. "I can't have help that's deaf, you know. Dr Prole is very particular that his instructions are followed to the letter, with every 'i' dotted and every 't' crossed, and that is my policy as well." She claps her hands. "Chop-chop, I can't be sitting here like a doorstop all evening, you know. We have to get you two sorted, don't we? Have to show you what to do."

Reluctantly, if resignedly, Kiki and Trish move from the door, and into the general gloom of the room. Feeling it to be both polite and useful to give Mrs Stump their names, Trish begins to speak, but gets no farther than "My na—".

"Oh, I don't need to be burdened with that nonsense." Mrs Stump waves her hand dismissively. "All my girls are Mary, and all my lads are James. Dr Prole has enough on his mind with all his medical knowledge and remembering everything that ever happened anywhere in the world since the beginning of time without having to recall the names of every child who comes to work for him." She narrows her eyes and purses her lips as though about to spit out a cherry pip. "Though I daresay none have been quite like you, and that's the truth." Mrs Stump shakes her head. "I thought I'd seen everything, for Dr Prole's not only one of the most eminent physicians in London, you know, he's a renowned traveller and explorer, always going off to some corner of the globe or other on his expeditions; collecting and studying everything that ever existed; but I'll wager he's never seen the likes of you two. Where on this good, green earth did you fetch from?" Her eyes darken warily and she puts a hand to her heart as a sinister thought enters her head. "Dear God, you aren't actors, are you?" The look of horror on her face and the shrill pitch of her voice are such that she might be asking if they are vicious criminals, wanted by the law. "Because I can't be having actors, you know, not in the house of a gentleman such as Dr Prole. That would never do. Never do at all."

Kiki and Trish, of course, come from a world where even very bad and talentless actors are treated like gods, and are, therefore, not a little surprised by this passionate outburst.

"What's wrong with actors, then?" asks Trish. Which proves not to be the best question she could have come up with.

"What's wrong with them?" Mrs Stump's eyes are now wide with shock and her voice so shrill that the lamp flame shivers. "What's right with them, that's what I'd like to know. There is nothing with legs that is lower on the face of the earth, not one solitary thing. Thieves, liars, fornicators, atheists and drunks, every last one of them."

"We aren't actors," Trish quickly assures her.

'I've never even been in a school play," adds Kiki.

Mrs Stump releases her hand from her chest. "Well praise the Lord in all His infinite wisdom and mercy for that." She picks up the lamp and moves it back and forth in front of them. "So where do you hale from, then? Bohemia? Styria? Kozep-Magyarorezag?" Her small eyes move back and forth and up and down with the lamp. "Moravia? Surely not Astrakhan?" Mrs Stump's lamp and gaze come to rest on Trish in her faded jeans, flannel shirt, denim jacket and trainers the pink of cheap candy (though, in this light, and given the day that they've had, they are more the colour of mud). Mrs Stump tilts her head to one side in thought. "America, perhaps? You do look like you might be from that frontier of theirs. From what I understand there is very little civilization to be found in that country – not as we know it, to be sure."

Of all the possible places of their origin that Mrs Stump has named, the only one either Kiki or Trish recognizes is America.

"America," says Kiki.

"That's right." Trish immediately agrees. "America."

"America…" Mrs Stump nods. "What did I say?"

"My father's a cowboy," embellishes Trish (who has enjoyed many a Western on lonely weekend afternoons).

"A cowboy?" Mrs Stump's eyes and lamp move to Kiki. "And what's your father, then? A Red Indian?"

"That's right," says Trish before Kiki can answer that his father is a minicab driver. "His father's a Red Indian. A chief. You know, with the feathers and the bows and arrows and all."

"Well, fancy that…" Mrs Stump's head and her lamp bob up and down. "And you're wearing shoes like anybody else might. I thought you people always went barefoot."

"Not in London." Kiki gives Trish a sour look. "In London we don't use bows and arrows, and we wear shoes."

Disappointed, perhaps, by the shoes and the lack of primitive armaments, Mrs Stump returns her attention to Trish and the lamp to its place on the table. "And what, if I may ask, are you two doing over here in the civilized world?"

"Well…" Trish has no idea what they're doing

over here. She glances at Kiki, but he, of course, has no idea either.

It is fortunate, then, that Mrs Stump does have one. "Don't tell me!" she says. "Your fathers are with one of those Wild West Shows."

Trish can't tell from Mrs Stump's tone whether or not she holds the same extremely low opinion of theatrical cowboys and Indians that she does of actors, but she fervently hopes not and takes a chance. "That's right. They're with a Wild West Show."

"And your mothers? Are they with the show as well?"

"Oh, yeah," says Trish, trying to think of something her mother could do in the Wild West Show. "My mother's a sharpshooter. And his dances. You know, for rain and things like that."

"And why aren't you with them, then?" Mrs Stump, it seems, is a woman of many questions.

"Were," says Kiki, thinking quickly. "They *were* in a Wild West Show. Only the—"

"Boat sank," fills in Trish, who recently watched the film *Titanic* on the telly. "Yeah, the boat sank on the way over to France and our parents all drowned, so we came back here. You know, where we can speak the language and all."

Mrs Stump, who has buried seven brothers and sisters, five children of her own, and Mr Stump himself, isn't unduly distressed by the news of their parents' tragic deaths. "I see... I see... Left you stranded without a penny, did they?" Much as Mr Stump left her. "Well, then..." Mrs Stump sits up very straight. "Let's get down to business, shall we? Do you understand what your duties are to be?"

Trish, of course, was not consulted about accepting Mrs Stump's offer of employment, but it should be mentioned here that she didn't take it seriously. The important thing to her was that it might get them off the streets for the night – and possibly even get them a meal to boot. Mrs Stump was clearly all wound up when she first saw them, and Trish assumed that, once she'd calmed down and had a good look at them, she would realize that, amongst other things, she and Kiki are much too young to work. Trish, therefore, is somewhat taken aback to discover that they aren't too young after all. "Pardon?"

"Your duties, girl. I told you. I need a maid-of-all-work and a boy for the house and stable and whatnot. Do you understand what these positions entail or not?"

Unlike Trish, Kiki is no stranger to the concept of child employment, and so manages to respond without showing any shock. "Not really," says Kiki.

"Not really, *Mrs Stump*," she corrects. "And Dr Prole is always 'Sir' to you. *Yes, Sir... No, Sir... Whatever you please, Sir...* Is that clear? Not that you're likely to see much of him of course – he is a very busy and important man, very important. Comes and goes like the wind." And sometimes like a tornado, she might add but doesn't. "But in the event that you do come across him, you always address him as 'Sir'. Is that understood? He is a proper gentleman, remember – not only because of his own nature and achievements, but because he is descended from one of the oldest families in the land. He has many friends in high places, you know – I daresay if you went to the ends of the earth you'd find kings and emperors who have dined with Dr Prole. So although you may hail from the Wild West you'll mind your manners while you're under this roof."

"Yes," mumbles Kiki, "Mrs Stump."

"You see? That wasn't too difficult, was it?" Mrs Stump gives him a curt nod. "Now, as to the work, I need a boy for a messenger and to run errands and do the heavy chores and see to the horses and carriage." In other words, to do the jobs of at least three grown men. She frowns. "You're a bit on the small side for lifting Dr Prole's crates and boxes, but we can always build you up, I suppose. And I assume that you can walk and run well enough – and look after the horses – being as you're a Red Indian. Is my assumption correct?"

Kiki nods. "Yes, Mrs Stump. I can walk and run all right – and look after the horses."

"Good." Mrs Stump turns back to Trish. "And what about you? Naturally, I do the shopping and cooking – Dr Prole is very particular about his food, very particular, as you would expect from a man who breaks bread with royalty and ministers on a regular basis – but I need a girl to do the general cleaning, polish the silver, see to the laundry, tend the fires and so forth." Maid-of-all-work being, obviously, a literal description.

Trish is frowning. "So I do everything you and Kiki don't do."

"His name is James," Mrs Stump reminds her. "And I won't have you taking that sulky tone with me, young lady." Displeasure does nothing to make Mrs Stump seem any warmer. "You should count yourself lucky that Dr Prole is a very progressive, forward-looking gentleman so that we have proper water closets here and you don't have to empty the slops. You should also be grateful that he is a single gentleman with no wife or children to be cared for. And, in any event, your duties are light enough if you ask me, being restricted to just this side of the house." It seems that Dr Prole's

190

living quarters take up only one-half of the double villa. The other half is given over to the private museum that houses his extensive and world-famous collections of antiquities and art. "He's got everything a soul can imagine in there," asserts Mrs Stump. And then some, she might add. Dr Prole's collection spans centuries across the entire globe. Statues and paintings, jewellery and vases, religious relics and icons, plates and coins and weaponry and every form of record-making ever known to man, from stone tablets to printed pages hand-bound in leather. "He's even got a mummy, would you believe?" adds Mrs Stump. "A real mummy, all the way from Egypt. I'm used to all the tombs and such he's got in the basement, but it gave me quite a turn when he brought that back with him. Quite a turn. Dr Prole's collection is worth the ransom of a dozen kings. More precious than Solomon's crown, most of it," intones Mrs Stump. "No one's allowed in there without a formal invitation – with the exception of me and Dr Prole, of course. I am the only one allowed to touch anything – ever – is that understood? Because I have his trust." She wags a finger at Trish. "Which you do not. So if you don't feel you're up to a bit of honest work, then there's more out on the street would be glad of a fine situation like this."

"It's not that, Mrs Stump," Trish hastens to reassure her. "It's just that, to tell you the truth, I'd much rather run errands than—"

"Run errands?" Mrs Stump's mouth twitches, but whether with amusement or outrage isn't quite clear. "I've never heard of such a thing in all my born days. That's not proper work for a girl." She purses her lips and eyes Trish coldly. "Am I to take it you are not capable of performing simple domestic chores?"

Trish quickly amends her position. "No, of course not. Mrs Stump. I do— I used to do things like that for my mum."

"Did you?" Mrs Stump's look is still as frosty as a day deep in winter. "Well, you might find this very different to what you are used to. This is a proper gentleman's house, you know, not a log cabin. Dr Prole likes it kept as though the Queen herself might drop by for tea." Though it is unlikely, of course, that her majesty would be permitted to touch any of his things either.

"I'm a very quick learner, Mrs Stump," answers Trish, who has given so little evidence of this in school that, were her teachers to hear her, quite a few eyebrows would be raised in astonishment.

"Are you?" Mrs Stump's bony fingers tap on the top of the table. Like most of us, Mrs Stump tends to believe what she wants to believe, and at

192

this moment Mrs Stump would very much like to believe Trish. A day without help is a day too long as far as she's concerned. "Well, you had better be. I don't imagine you've ever been in a proper house like this before, so let me tell you the first rule of getting on with ladies and gentlemen." Mrs Stump moves her finger in an instructive way. "You don't see anything, you don't hear anything, and you don't say anything – not ever. It's not for you to meddle in the business of your betters. Is that understood?"

"Yes, Mrs Stump," say Trish and Kiki.

"Very well, then. We shall try you out." Mrs Stump rises. "Where are your bags? I'll show you where you sleep."

"We don't have any bags," says Kiki.

"No bags? All the way from America without any bags?"

"They were lost," says Trish. "You know, at sea. They went down with the boat."

"I see." Mrs Stump looks them up and down. "Well, it seems that this is, indeed, your lucky day. Since they went off so sudden, your predecessors left some garments behind that should fit you well enough. We can't have you going about like that, can we?" Without interrupting the flow of her words, she reclaims the lamp and passes back through the kitchen door. "I don't know what Dr

Prole would say if he saw you got up like that."
She starts down the narrow basement hall once
more. "We'll have no further mention of the Wild
West. No mention at all."

Mrs Stump herself has a small apartment on the
top floor, but Kiki and Trish are to sleep in the
two very basic rooms that share this half of the
basement with the kitchen. Kiki has the cupboard-
like room at the very front of the house and Trish
has the cupboard-like room beside it. Above
stairs, Dr Prole's house is opulently carpeted and
furnished, but in these rooms there is merely a
narrow cot, a pair of hooks on the wall, a shelf
and a tiny table containing a candleholder and
part of a candle (which Mrs Stump is good enough
to light, though with the warning that they are not
to waste it needlessly). Only Trish's room has a
fireplace, and that has been blocked off, which,
from the point of view of keeping warm, makes it
fortunate that the room is so small.

Mrs Stump leaves them to go back to the
kitchen to organize the chores that must be done
before they have their evening meal, and to give
them a chance to change into "proper" clothes. As
soon as Trish has put on the plain and patched
grey dress left behind by her "predecessor" (a girl
much taller and heavier than Trish) she slips from
her room and into Kiki's.

"You could've knocked," grumbles Kiki, hastily pulling his predecessor's worn brown trousers up over his predecessor's rough wool shirt.

"And you could've kept your big mouth shut," snaps Trish. "Why did you go and tell her we'd work for her?"

The answer to this is a simple one, of course – though not the simple one involving getting a room for the night that Trish was expecting.

"Because Mrs Calabash told me to."

"Crikey!" Trish rolls her eyes, but it is a fairly futile gesture considering the darkness of the room. "You really think that cat can talk to you."

"Not in words," says Kiki. "But it's like I said before, Mrs Calabash is here to help us, so I reckon we should listen to her."

"Then it's too bad we don't know where she is, isn't it?" snipes Trish.

"Yes we do." Kiki points behind her. "She's on my bed."

Trish turns round. It is only just possible to make out a darker patch on the darkness of the cot, but at that moment the dark patch opens its golden eyes and looks straight at her.

Staring into Mrs Calabash's eyes can be a disquieting experience, so Trish looks at Kiki. "But how did she get there?"

Kiki shrugs. "I don't know. I saw her as soon as

Mrs Stump went off." He doesn't add that he had the distinct impression that Mrs Calabash was smiling.

"And what does she say about the mess you got us into?" demands Trish.

"Me? You're the one who said she can do housework."

"Well I can," says Trish with more confidence than might actually be warranted. "I help my mum, don't I? I cook and do the hoovering and all. And, anyway, I only said that because you said you could walk and run and handle the horses! What was I meant to do, go back on the street on my own?"

"I *can* handle the horses," says Kiki.

Trish does a passable impersonation of the animal under discussion. "Oh, right, course you can. And where do you keep your horses on the sixteenth floor? On the blinkin' balcony?"

"I didn't always live on the sixteenth floor," he replies. "My grandfather had a horse. And I wouldn't've let that happen – you know, you going back on the street on your own. I would've gone with you."

Trish, who has never really had anyone to depend on before but herself, doesn't know how to react to this declaration of solidarity and so chooses to ignore it. "Well, whoever's fault it is, we're here now."

"But why? That's what we have to ask ourselves," says Kiki. "Why are we here?"

Trish scowls at the grim little room. "Because we're being punished for some terrible thing we don't know we did, that's why."

Kiki tucks his shirt tails into his trousers. "You know what I think?"

Trish closes her eyes. It's been a very long day, but it seems to be getting even longer. "No, Kiki. What do you think?"

"I think we're here because we're meant to be helping Betty Friedman. That's why she made us promise to look after Mrs Calabash. Because Mrs Calabash knows what to do."

"Really?" Trish is so distracted by all the different thoughts in her head that she can only call up a fraction of the scorn she is feeling at the moment. "And what does Mrs Calabash say we should do now?"

But it is neither Kiki nor Mrs Calabash who speaks next.

"What are you two doing down there?" shouts Mrs Stump. "Hurry up! There's a lot to do tonight, you know. A lot to do."

"Well, I guess that answers that question," says Trish.

Mrs Stump Seems to Be the Only One without a Suspicious Nature

Neither Trish nor Kiki has had any opportunity to give further consideration to the questions of why they are in Dr Prole's house or what they are meant to do now that they are here, as they haven't had a moment to think since Mrs Stump called them to their chores last night. After they'd done those chores they were given a meagre supper of soup and a piece of bread, and then were sent to bed. Bed, however, was not a place they were destined to stay very long, the day of servants apparently beginning so early that Kiki and Trish have got to see precisely how dark it is before the dawn.

Trish's first job this morning was to clear and clean the fireplaces and lay the fires ready for lighting in all but Dr Prole's private chambers, as he came in late and doesn't wish to be disturbed. After that, Mrs Stump wanted her to start on the wash. "Sure," said Trish. "Where's the machine?" Mrs Stump said she didn't know what went on in America, but over here the only machine they have is Trish herself. "Oh, right," muttered Trish. "I forgot." Mrs Stump sniffed. Now Kiki has been sent off to the stables, leaving Trish polishing silver under Mrs Stump's watchful eye while they wait for Dr Prole to leave the house.

"There's no sense in starting your instruction proper while Dr Prole's still here and needs my attention," says Mrs Stump. "As soon as he's gone we'll start with the washing." She scowls at Trish. "I can see very well it will take me hours to teach you how to do just that."

"Yes, Mrs Stump," mumbles Trish.

"It ought to have been done yesterday," Mrs Stump gives another of her disapproving sniffs, "if the girl hadn't run off like that. That was the second girl I've lost in less than a week, can you believe it? They don't usually leave as quick as that." Mrs Stump pours herself another cup of tea. "The one before was here for months. There were a few tears, mind you, but no accidents or mistakes that came to the doctor's attention. Dr Prole, he doesn't tolerate accidents or mistakes."

Listening to Mrs Stump's conversation is a bit like standing on the bank, watching a river rush by – carrying along with it every leaf and twig that has happened to fall in. Trish says, "Um…"

"It was a shame she left like that," Mrs Stump continues. "Things were going so well. And then, sudden as a shower, she comes and says she's decided to go. Said she'd arranged for her cousin to take her place. I didn't even know she *had* a cousin, being an orphan and all, but she said her cousin had references from a lord and was looking for a good position with someone of a similar station." Mrs Stump stirs a spoonful of sugar into her tea.

"But she didn't have references from no lord, did she?" guesses Trish.

"Indeed she did." Mrs Stump lays her spoon in the saucer. "Which is what swung it for me, as you can well imagine. Even though I had a feeling about her right from the start. But if she was good enough for a lord, then she was good enough for Dr Prole, that's what I told myself." She lifts her cup and takes a sip of her tea. "After all, he saved my life, he did, there's no doubt about that. Saved my life as surely as if he'd pulled me from a burning building," declares Mrs Stump. "After Mr Stump up and left this vale of tears so unexpected, I would have ended my days in the workhouse if it hadn't been for Dr Prole. Everything I've got, I owe to him." Which, considering how she skims money off the household expenses, is certainly true. "I'd do anything for him, I swear. Anything at all." And this is also true. Her loyalty, as Dr Prole well knows, is beyond question or reproach. "But, as I said, as soon as I set eyes on her I had the feeling that she was trouble. Something about her eyes. Had a touch of the other about them, if you know what I mean. Made me uneasy, they did. And she refused to let me call her Mary, can you believe it? Acted like a proper madam. Said her name was Constance and that was all she'd answer to. Constance! If ever a girl was mis-named, she was the one. I should have known she'd come to no good." Mrs Stump shakes her head at her own credulity. "Still, Dr Prole didn't blame me in the least. Not in the least. Not even when she got into his study. I could hardly believe it. In his study! No wonder he was so upset. That's why she left like that. She thought he wasn't to return for hours, didn't she? So she nipped into his study and was helping herself to whatever when he came back unexpected. Practically caught her red-handed. So she ran out through the basement without taking her things or her wretched cat."

Trish looks up. One or two things that aren't leaves or twigs in the river of Mrs Stump's mono-logue have finally caught her attention. "She had a cat?"

Mrs Stump sighs. "I told you that yesterday.

Don't you listen to a word I say?"

Trish, who has listened to as few of Mrs Stump's words as possible, now realizes that this was a mistake. "It's just that a lot happened yesterday. I remember now she had a cat." She bends her head again and rubs a little harder at the spoon in her hand. "But I didn't know she was thieving." Her head still bent to her task, Trish glances over at the housekeeper. "What did she nick? I thought studies just have books in them."

"'Tis true. Books and all his papers, mainly. And I'm sure I don't know what she took. Only she and Dr Prole know that. But some of those books and old maps and the like are very valuable." Mrs Stump sighs into her teacup. "Worth a bob or two whatever it was, I'll tell you that. He was out searching for her half the night. But she vanished into thin air like the devil himself."

Her interest rising, Trish no longer feels the numbness or the aching in her hands. "What about the police?" she asks. Dr Prole being so famous and respected and all, she reckons he must have some friends pretty high up in the constabulary.

"Police?" snaps Mrs Stump. "It was an accident what happened to the boy. There was no need for the police."

"No, I meant about the robbery. What did the

police say about that?"

"Oh, no. No police." Mrs Stump shakes her head. "Dr Prole, he didn't feel there was a need to drag them into it. Said a prayer for her soul would be more productive."

"He did?" When Trish's mother's bag was nicked on the tube that time she didn't pray, she was screaming for revenge. "But I thought you said he was in such a state and—"

Mrs Stump's small mouth becomes even smaller. "Of course he was in a state. Wouldn't you be if someone you let into your very home did a thing like that? Just think what might have happened if he hadn't left something behind and had to return."

Trish is beginning to imagine that very thing.

"But unlike some of us," continues Mrs Stump with a look at Trish, "Dr Prole has an exceedingly kind and charitable heart."

"Really?" Although she has yet to meet Dr Prole, Trish already knows that this isn't true. Trish suspects that if Dr Prole didn't set the police on Constance, it was because he'd already dealt with her himself – not because he preferred to save her soul.

"Yes, *really*," says Mrs Stump. "Why do you think he set up his hospital all out of his own pocket? It's not like he has nothing else to do. It's not like he needs what little profit it may bring him. No, he did it because he cares about the suffering of his fellows, that's why."

One of the bells lined up against the kitchen wall begins to ring demandingly, cutting short Mrs Stump's morning monologue. Dr Prole has risen to begin his day of selfless and tireless work.

"Lawksadaisy! Is it that time already? And him not come in till all hours." Mrs Stump jumps to her feet so quickly that she knocks her spoon to the floor and nearly topples the cup as well.

Trish looks up in surprise. It hadn't occurred to her before that Mrs Stump's respect and admiration for her employer contains an element of fear.

Kiki steers Dr Prole's sleek, black carriage – drawn by two equally sleek and black horses – to a stop in front of Number 33, and pushes his hat out of his eyes, unsure whether he's meant to tell Mrs Stump that he is here or simply wait. Rain falls on the elegant houses and gravelled road of the square, on the shrubs and trees of the central garden, and on Kiki Monjate as he sits in the driver's seat of the landau, protected only by an old Macintosh of Mr Stump's that would easily accommodate two small boys and a worn and dented top hat that once belonged to the great man himself, and that, presumably, hadn't constantly slid down the great man's forehead.

Kiki's day has not started well. He awoke expecting Mrs Calabash to be sleeping beside him, but sometime in the night she left his side and went into hiding. As long as Mrs Calabash is near, Kiki feels safe. Without her, he and Trish have only themselves to rely on – which Kiki very much fears may not be enough. He knows that Mrs Calabash will both tell them what to do and protect them from harm. But there was no time to look for her. He had taken no more than a sip of his morning tea when Mrs Stump sent him to the mews behind the house to see to the horses.

"You'd better get cracking, Dr Prole will be wanting to leave for the hospital as soon as he's finished his breakfast," she informed him. "You'd best get all the blood off the carriage before you bring it round, as well."

Already exhausted from his pre-dawn chores, Kiki thought he hadn't heard her right. "The blood?"

"Your predecessor's blood," Mrs Stump elaborated. "From when he got himself killed the other night."

"Coo," said Kiki. "I thought he ran off."

Mrs Stump took two loaves of freshly baked bread from the oven. "That was the girl. The boy fell off the carriage and ran himself over."

Now, as the rain continues to pour down, Kiki is thinking that perhaps he should tell Mrs Stump that he is here when the front door opens and Dr Prole steps through it, his handsome face tight with irritation. At the sight of him, Kiki feels the fear that most adults produce in him, but if it weren't for the poor visibility afforded by the weather that fear would be much greater. For although Dr Prole is a handsome man (and, judging by his clothes, also as rich and important as Mrs Stump claims), he is not a particularly nice one, no matter how generous and Christian he likes to appear – which is something someone as sensitive as Kiki would recognize right away.

"Here you are at last, James." He snaps open a black umbrella and holds it over his head. "It's a wonder I haven't grown grey waiting. What took you so long?"

"I'm sorry, Sir." Kiki tips his hat the way he's seen humble servants do in costume dramas on the telly – but decides against mentioning the difficulty he had in removing his predecessor's blood from the wheels. "I had a bit of bother putting up the roof."

"Did you?" Dr Prole opens the carriage door, not once having actually glanced in Kiki's direction. "And can I assume that you know where we're going, or are you planning to have a bit of bother with that as well?"

"The hospital," says Kiki. "I know the way." Because of the steady turnover in domestic help, Mrs Stump has provided him with a small note-book covered in oilskin that contains directions to and from all the places Dr Prole usually frequents, as well as maps.

"Then see if you can't get us there before the end of the century. I have a busy day ahead of me." Dr Prole collapses his umbrella, climbs into the landau, and slams shut the door.

Kiki drives slowly, partly because the further they go the more the rain has turned the roads to mud, and partly because he has to pull the oilskin-covered notebook from his jacket from time to time to check the way. But it is a long journey no matter how fast one drives, for Dr Prole's hospital, though created because of his concern for suffer-ing humanity, is, in fact, located as far from most humanity as it can be.

At last they cross a small river and begin to ascend the rather steep hill to the hospital. At the crest of the hill is an imposing, wrought iron entrance gate and, behind it, the grey-brick edifice of the hospital itself.

The gatekeeper unlocks and opens the massive gate as the carriage approaches.

"Morning, Dr Prole, Sir," he says as the landau

passes him. "Frightful weather, ain't it, Sir?"

If Dr Prole responds, Kiki doesn't hear him.

Kiki has been so occupied with one thing or another for the past several hours that he has totally forgotten about making his usual charms to protect himself against the invisible forces of the universe, but the sight of Dr Prole's hospital reminds him. A dark building, made almost black by the rain, there is nothing about it that suggests welcome. There is nothing to tell you its name or purpose; no signs or directions to the various wards and departments; no stall selling flowers to cheer up the ill. Also, possibly because of the many closed shutters and the bars on every window, there is nothing about it that suggests that, once you have entered, you are ever likely to leave.

The horses trudge up the circular drive through the gravel and mud. As soon as they come to a stop in front of the stone steps that lead to the main entrance, the porter rushes out of his kiosk, carrying an umbrella to save Dr Prole the inconvenience of having to unfurl his own.

"Good morning, Dr Prole," says the porter, opening the carriage door. "Frightful weather, ain't it, Sir?"

Dr Prole grunts, but, although the porter takes this as agreement, it is only an indication of the effort needed to climb out of the landau. "I shan't be long, James," he calls. "Wait for me here." And, the porter trotting beside him holding the umbrella over his head, he hurries up the stairs.

Kiki watches Dr Prole disappear inside. Where it is warm and dry, and where there is probably a nice, hot cup of tea waiting for him – possibly with a biscuit or bun to go with it.

The minutes pass, and then the tens of minutes – Dr Prole's "shan't be long" proving to be rather optimistic. Huddled into Mr Stump's old Mac, Kiki crosses his fingers and taps his tongue against the roof of his mouth, giving some serious thought to his employer for the first time. As naive as it may seem, until this moment it hadn't occurred to Kiki to be suspicious of the man in whose house he and Trish find themselves. He believed that they are on the path Betty Friedman has set for them, but he didn't think that the path might end with Erasmus Prole, he thought it simply passed his door. Now, however, it does occur to him. Does Dr Prole, renowned collector of antiquities that he is, have the documents that Betty Friedman hoped were in the church? If he does have them, does he know their importance? If he does have them, where might they be?

Kiki's brain is sinking under these thoughts much as his coat and hat are sinking under the weight of the rain, when he's suddenly aware that someone is trying to get his attention. He looks towards the entrance.

The porter is standing at the door of the lodge, beckoning. "James!" he calls. "James! Come on in here where you can watch the horses, lad, and have a cup of tea before you catch your death!"

The porter's tiny lodge, heated by a small brazier, is warm as well as dry. The porter's name is Mr Jax.

"Can't have you sitting out there like a post." Mr Jax pours out a cup of tea from a battered kettle. "No telling how long your guv'nor will be. Time don't mean the same to the likes of him as to you and me."

Kiki takes the cup, grateful just for the heat of it against his hands. "You mean because he might have to operate on someone or something like that?"

"That ain't likely." The porter laughs, which is the first time in quite a while that Kiki has heard that sound. "Not in a place like this."

"I thought it was a hospital," says Kiki.

The porter smiles. "You're new, ain't you?" He gives Kiki a friendly wink. "Sometimes I think your guv'nor changes his lads more often than I change my socks."

"So what is it if it's not a hospital?"

The porter takes up his own cup of tea.

"Madhouse, ain't it?" Which explains the bars. "As you would know if you was the boy brought him here the other evening with that girl. Fit to be tied, she was. Fit to be tied. Carrying on about demons and wizards and such all the while they were dragging her inside. Even accused your guv'nor of stealing something off her – like she had anything worth stealing by even a common buzman. 'It don't belong to you,' she was screaming. 'None of it belongs to you. You're killing time, that's what you're doing. You're killing time.' Mad as they come."

Kiki leans forward, afraid to trust either his ears or his luck. "Killing time? Are you sure that's what she said?"

"Course I'm sure. I've got the hearing of a bat. That's what she said." The porter shakes his head. "This place has its share of Egyptian queens and King Arthurs and even a chap who thinks he's Jesus Christ, but I never heard nothing the likes of that before."

Trying to hide his excitement, Kiki takes another gulp of tea before he says, "What was she like – the girl Dr Prole brought in the other night?"

The porter shrugs. "Your usual sort of girl, I'd say. Not from his regular class of patient, though. Not the way she was dressed." Dr Prole's hospital, he explains, is an exclusive, private establishment for the care and treatment of people from wealthy families whose reason has left them like rats deserting a sinking ship. "That's why it's way out here, ain't it? You don't want Lord So-and-So to be reminded of his poor old sister who howls at the moon every time he looks out his window, do you?" Mr Jax shakes his head. "No, I daresay she's one of his charity cases." He lowers his voice and winks. "The rich may own everything else, but they don't own the rights on going mad."

As if in answer the voice of Erasmus Prole booms out, "James! James! Why aren't you with the horses?"

Kiki and the porter slam their cups down on the table in guilt and surprise.

"I was just coming, Sir." Kiki jumps to his feet and opens the door of the lodge, but Dr Prole, too annoyed even to wait for help, is already marching down the steps so sharply that it looks as if the rain parts around him. Kiki turns back to the tiny room. "Can you remember what she was wearing?" he asks.

The porter blinks. "Wearing?"

"The girl," whispers Kiki, afraid, somehow, that Dr Prole will hear him. "Can you remember what she was wearing?"

"'Twas a dress, of course," replies the porter. "A blue dress."

Taking Some Initiative

It is late in the night and the house is dark and still, which can be considered a small mercy in an unkind world. A world whose background sounds consist not of music or sirens or honking horns, but a litany of criticisms and orders. *Glory lawksamercy, you couldn't move slower if you were bolted to the floor... you're a wonder of nature, you are, all thumbs and no digits... mind that fire... black this... polish that... fetch that bucket... groom the horses... scrub the floor... sort those clothes... mend these sheets... sweep the steps... deliver this... collect that...* Indeed, it would be fair to say that until they joined Dr Prole's establishment, Kiki and Trish never really understood the meaning of either the word "exhausted" or the word "work". The endless stream of tasks and the constant, nagging presence of Mrs Stump, watching them as if they're the chain gang and she's its boss, has made it impossible for them to have even a minute alone together all day. Which is why, instead of collapsing in well-deserved sleep, they are settling themselves on Kiki's cot with the snoring Mrs Calabash between them.

"Wait'll I tell you! Wait'll I tell you!" Trish is as excited as a girl on the verge of physical collapse can be. "I found out all this stuff this morning from Old Boot Face. About my *predecessor* and why she ran off and all. And you're right! It all fits! Everything!" It's impossible to bounce on the board that is Kiki's bed, so Trish hugs herself instead. "You want to know what I think, Kiki?"

But Kiki already knows.

"You think Dr Prole's the bloke in your dream – the bloke we saw the other night."

"What?" Even in the feeble light of their stump of candle, he can see the surprise on Trish's face. But she doesn't wait for his answer. "And anyway, that's not all. My predecessor – Constance?"

"She's the girl in the blue dress."

"Go on!" Trish gives him a shove. "How do you know that?"

Kiki grins. "Because I know where she is."

"You what?"

"I know where she is."

Trish sighs impatiently. "Well, where is she?"

"She's in Dr Prole's hospital." And, finally given a chance to speak himself, Kiki tells Trish about the asylum and the mad girl Dr Prole brought in two nights ago.

"But that's brilliant!" Trish is hugging herself again. "'Cos I reckon that bundle she was carrying was the documents. She nicked them from Dr Prole's study. Only he caught her, didn't he? So she never had a chance to hide them in the crypt like she meant to."

"Who do you think the girl in blue is, then?" asks Kiki.

Trish frowns. "What?"

"Who's the girl in blue?" Kiki rubs Mrs Calabash behind her ears – more to comfort himself than to comfort her. "I mean, she can't be just some ordinary girl, can she?"

Mrs Calabash's tail slaps against Trish's thigh. "Why don't you tell me what *you* think?"

"I think she must be a Time Keeper. Mr Jax said she was screaming about killing time, right? And if she took the documents and was trying to hide them in the church—"

"Then she knew how important they are." Trish nods. "That's good, Kiki. That makes sense." She nods again. "So everything really is going according to plan."

"But it doesn't really help, does it?" asks Kiki.

"What do you mean it doesn't help? Of course it helps." They've been stumbling along, following Mrs Calabash, but Trish can see that it is now time to finally follow Betty Friedman's advice and take the initiative. "All we've got to do is talk to Constance. I bet she can tell us where the documents are."

Trish's enthusiasm, however, is not shared by Kiki. "So how do you plan to do that? Just walk in and ask to see her?"

He meant this suggestion to be sarcastic, but Trish nods happily. "Exactly." Once again, Trish's extensive knowledge of the world as seen through the television screen has come to her aid. "I'll say I'm her sister and came for a visit. Even madhouses let visitors in. I saw it in this story on the telly."

Kiki stares at her in silence for a second or two, uncertain whether the feeling she inspires in him is awe or terror. He decides that it's terror. "And what if he's killed her?" Dr Prole, Kiki reckons, is not a man you want to cross.

Trish sighs. "But he didn't kill her, did he? She's in the asylum. The porter told you so."

"That doesn't mean she's still alive," argues Kiki. "And anyway what if he kills you?" The thought of the doors of Dr Prole's asylum shutting on Trish is enough to freeze his heart. "Or locks you up, too?"

It is easier to be brave if you are someone like Trish, who never stops to think about the consequences of her actions, rather than someone like Kiki, who does.

"He's not going to kill me," says Trish. "And he's not going to lock me up, neither. I'll take Mrs Calabash along. You said she makes you feel safe, right? Well then, Mrs Calabash will protect me, won't she? She'll be my guardian cat."

A new thought occurs to Kiki, one that is both terrifying and comforting at the same time. "And how are you going to get there? It's not just round the corner, you know."

"How do you think? You'll take me."

What is comforting about this is that it means he will be on hand to help Trish; what is terrifying is that it means that they may both get caught.

"What about Mrs Stump?" It seems to Kiki that Mrs Stump may be the only hope of discouraging Trish from her plan. "We can't stop to breathe for a minute without her finding something else for us to do. There's no way she's going to let both of us out of her sight for more than two seconds."

"She can't stay in all the time," reasons Trish. "We just have to wait till she goes out."

Which turns out to be not as far in the future as Kiki might have liked.

* * *

It may be coincidence (or it may be something else entirely), but, as it happens, the next day is Dr Prole's day in the City – where he meets with other important businessmen and dines at his club – which means that once Kiki has dropped Dr Prole off he is free to return to the house and stay there until late in the evening when it is time to fetch him back home. It also means that, since no supper must be provided, it is Mrs Stump's half-day off as well. Quite often she spends this time in her room with her needlepoint or knitting, but today she has taken herself out for a wander through the shops and a proper tea in a good restaurant. Mrs Stump believes that, in her absence, Trish and Kiki will be seeing to the many chores devised by her and God to keep the Devil from finding work for them, but Mrs Stump, as it happens, is wrong.

The reality is that Kiki and Trish left the house not long after she did, and now, as Mrs Stump, in her second-best hat and cloak, stops to admire a pair of boots in a shop window, Trish is climbing down from Dr Prole's carriage at the bottom of the hill on which the hospital sits.

Kiki carefully hands a covered wicker basket down to her. Often, it is more terrifying to think about doing something than it is to actually do it. This is certainly true for Kiki, who is now feeling a lot better about Trish's plan than he felt last night.

Though not one hundred per cent better. He is still worried that leaving the hospital may prove more difficult than entering. "If you're not out in an hour, I'm coming after you, right?"

"You've got to give me longer than that." Trish, of course, has no worries at all. She slips the basket over her arm. "I mean, what if it takes me a while to convince them to let me see her? Or she's sleeping? Or the bloke who's in charge is having his lunch?"

"An hour and ten minutes, then," concedes Kiki. "But not a minute more."

"An hour and a half," says Trish, and without further consultation, she marches boldly up the hill

Trish's confidence is partly based on ignorance. It isn't until she walks through the gate that she has her first clear view of the hospital that Dr Prole built because he cares so much about the suffering of his fellows – and understands Kiki's concern. "It gave me a fright when I saw it," Kiki had told her – and it gives Trish a fright as well. If The Wat is hopelessness given form and substance in concrete, Dr Prole's asylum is hopelessness given form and substance in brick.

Inside the basket, Mrs Calabash purrs softly.

"You're right," whispers Trish. "The sooner we go in, the sooner we'll get out again," and she lifts her chin and marches straight across the lawn.

The name of the bloke who's in charge of the asylum turns out to be Matron Earp. Matron Earp is a large, formidable and rather looming woman with the bearing and manner of a battlefield general.

"This is most unusual." Matron Earp is also a woman whose occupation and nature have joined forces to make certain that she never smiles. "Normally visitors make appointments in advance."

But as formidable and looming as she is, Matron Earp holds little terror for a girl who's been raised by the ex-Mrs O'Leary. Not only is Matron Earp sober but, because of her vocation, she takes obvious pride in her own sanity and reasonableness.

"I know this is a little unexpected," says Trish, "but I thought that, since I was passing by with the shopping –" she taps the lidded basket on her lap – "you know, that maybe it would be all right if I could just see Constance for a few minutes. So I know she's all right. I mean, she *is* my sister."

"Constance?" Matron Earp frowns as though the number of women named Constance amongst the inmates is so great that it is difficult for her to tell them apart. "Constance what?"

"Oh, you must know her. Constance. She's got

bright red hair and she was wearing a blue dress?" Trish smiles hopefully back at Matron Earp's ferocious gaze. "Dr Prole said he brought her in three nights ago," she says, without actually claiming that it was to her that he said this. "She made a right stink. Accused him of stealing from her and all. That's the thanks he gets for being so kind. But she never was the grateful sort."

"Oh … Constance. The charity case…" Matron Earp, now under the impression that Trish has been sent by Dr Prole himself, finally displays an expression that is not disapproval. "Here we call her Mary." She nods. "Of course you may see her. Though not for more than five minutes – and not that it'll do you much good, mind. Not in the state she's in."

"She's that mad?" asks Trish.

"Oh, she's that mad." Matron Earp takes a large ring of keys from her desk, gets up, and walks towards the door. It's like watching a mountain move. "Which is why we've had to give her something to calm her down. It was awful how she carried on. Your sister may look like a slip of a girl but, believe me, you could knock out ten men with what it took to quieten her." Matron Earp pauses with her hand on the doorknob. "So you understand that she may not make very much sense."

Trish doesn't consider this a problem. As far as she can tell, people, especially adults, rarely make much sense at the best of times. "I just want to see her." She picks up the basket and follows the nurse into the corridor. "You know, for Mum's sake."

"Your mother?" Matron Earp looks back at her and raises an eyebrow. "I didn't think Mary had a mother."

I could say the same for you, thinks Trish, but aloud only murmurs, "Oh, yes. We both do."

"I see," says Matron Earp, and, keys jangling, strides down the hall.

If there is anything good to be said about Dr Prole's hospital, it is that it is a model of organization and efficiency. The padded cells and dunking baths are in the basement where the violent and dangerous patients reside, kept down below the ground where there is little chance of sunlight or moonlight causing a fit – and little chance, as well, of anyone hearing them scream. The three main floors are occupied by the more docile and harmless of the inmates – the Egyptian queens, military heroes, saviours and the like who pass their days in worlds far more pleasant than the one they're actually in. In this section, the men and women each have a dining room and a communal room for recreation and socializing, as well as several small dormitories. At the very top, where the windows are small and the ceiling low, is where Dr Prole's special charity cases reside.

It is to the top floor, therefore, that Matron Earp leads Trish.

There is no dining or communal space up here. There is only a gloomy hallway, flanked on either side by narrow cells sealed by heavy doors, with small, barred holes at their centres.

"Dr Prole says it isn't good for them to fraternize," Matron Earp explains as she re-locks the door to the hallway behind them. "They're too far gone." She stops at the very first door, and peers through the square of bars. Inside the cell, a voice can be heard, talking to itself, "As awake as can be expected." She steps back, flicking through the ring of keys for the one she wants. "Mary," she says as she unlocks the cell. "Mary, you've got yourself a visitor. Look who's here."

"They've been stolen…" Constance is saying. "The stories told by stars… The dreams born at sunrise…"

Matron Earp looks round at Trish. "Pay her no mind," she advises. "It's the drugs. She's in another world." Then she says loudly, as though Constance is deaf as well as mad, "Mary, your sister's come to see you. Isn't that nice?"

"My sisters are in the wind," murmurs Constance.

Matron Earp grabs hold of Trish's arm and more or less yanks her inside.

Constance sits on the narrow bed that is the only furniture in the tiny room. Her hair is the colour of a new penny and her eyes the colour of a tropical sea, but there is no life in either of them now. The hair is dull and matted; the eyes empty and unseeing. Her blue dress has been replaced by a plain, grey shift.

"Never mind them," snaps Matron Earp. "They're nothing but air. This sister here is flesh and blood. And she's come all this way just to see you're all right." She gives Trish a none-too-gentle shove forward. "I'll be outside the door if you need me. I'll tell you when your time is up."

Because Constance's image has been with her since her dream, Trish almost feels as if she really is her sister – or at least a friend. This makes it easy for her to approach the other girl. "Constance," Trish whispers, taking the few steps needed to reach the bed. "Constance, can you hear me? Constance, it's me."

"Hooshtah... Hooshtah..." says Constance. "You can never find a camel when you need one."

"Constance. Constance, it's me, your sister Trish." She sits beside her on the bed. "What are you doing here? Mum is so worried."

"I always come. To be near the grave of him I so

224

dearly loved. To see the child. I come to be certain all is well." A single tear runs down her cheek. "But all wasn't well. It was gone," she whispers. "I thought my heart would break again. When I got to the vestry, the box was gone. And everything in it. After all those years. Safe for all those years. I had to get them back. I could see that loathsome man... I could see him having the box removed, and when I saw the sign... When I saw the sign, I knew who he was. I knew how to find him to get it back."

"I know who he is, too." Trish takes something from her pocket and puts it on the girl's lap. "Look. I brought your glove. I know what happened. I saw everything."

Constance looks down at the glove. "Did I drop it on the road? Or at the church? I can't remember... I was hurrying to get to the crypt."

"I know. But you didn't make it. Dr Prole caught up with you." Trish lowers her voice so that she herself can barely hear it. "That's what I've got to talk to you about. I—"

Constance laughs. "But I found them. He took them and I found them. I was going to the crypt..."

"Constance, please." Trish squeezes her knee beneath the grey shift. "I've really got to talk to you."

"Hooshtah... Hooshtah..." Constance's eyes suddenly focus on Trish. "Is it time to go?"

Trish glances over her shoulder, but Matron Earp has her back to the door. "No. Not yet. First I need to know what happened to the documents. The ones you took from Dr Prole."

Constance looks around nervously. "We have to get away. We have to hurry."

"I know we do. But first you have to try to think. Please. What happened to the documents?"

Constance shakes her head as though answering a question – though not the one Trish would like her to answer. "There is no future without a past."

"I know," says Trish. "I know that's true. Which is why you have to tell me where the documents are."

Constance picks up the glove and holds it in her hand. When her gaze comes back to Trish her eyes are no longer empty. "Who are you?" She looks at the basket on Trish's lap. "What's in there?"

"I'm Trish," Trish answers. Twisting round so the basket can't be seen from the door, she opens the wooden lid a crack. Mrs Calabash's head rises up in the opening. "And this is Mrs Calabash. We want to help you. But you've got to tell me where the documents are."

Constance fixes her stare on Mrs Calabash. Mrs Calabash begins to purr. The cat's soothing sound

226

and the glow of her golden eyes have their effect. Blinking for the first time since Trish has been with her, Constance sits up a little straighter, her own eyes widening and beginning to sparkle like the sea that they so resemble on a sunny day. "Catawampus…" says Constance, her voice low, but strong and clear. She turns to Trish, studying her face as though she really does know her. "You must be from the future."

"That's right," whispers Trish. "I am." She thinks Constance is starting to remember, and leans forward, expecting to be told where the documents are.

In which expectation, as in so many others, she is sadly mistaken.

"My cat!" Constance's eyes stay on Mrs Calabash, but she is seeing something that is happening only in her memory. "My cat!" she wails. "He killed my cat." She bursts into tears.

"What's going on in there?" Matron Earp jerks open the door. "Now look what you've done. You've set her off."

"No I didn't!" Trish protests. "It was the cat. You know, 'cos Constance loves her so much."

"Cat? Cat?" Suddenly, she is standing over Trish. "What is this?" demands Matron Earp. "Who said you could bring a cat in here?"

Since the answer to the matron's first question is

fairly obvious, and the answer to the second "no one", Trish answers a question she hasn't been asked. "I— It's her cat. I thought it might remind her of home."

"There are no animals allowed in here!" Matron Earp, though several stone heavier than Mrs Stump and not as charming, does have the fact that she is afraid of Dr Prole in common with the housekeeper. "Never! Do you hear me?" She snatches the basket from Trish's hands.

At the very moment Mrs Calabash leaps clear and races from the room.

Although not built for speed, Matron Earp runs after her.

Trish jumps to her feet to follow.

"Wait." Constance, wiping tears from her eyes with the blue glove, puts the other hand on Trish's. "Who are you? What do you want?"

"I'm a friend," answers Trish. "I'm from the future. So's the cat. And I want to know where the documents are. You know, the ones you took from Dr Prole."

"I can't tell you." Constance shakes her head. "I don't know. I only remember reaching the church. I don't know what happened to them after that."

"Out!" Matron Earp's bootsteps thud along the corridor. "I want you and that animal out of here this instant!"

Defeated, Trish slowly starts towards the door.

"But I can tell you where they were," says Constance.

Is the Light at the End of the Tunnel Only an Oncoming Train?

Going home. That is the thought uppermost in Trish and Kiki's minds since Trish's visit to Constance: they're going home. Trish can see herself sprawled on the sofa in front of the telly, while her mother mutters grievances and drinks cheap wine. It may not be an image of what most of us would consider domestic bliss, but it is for Trish. It is certainly an improvement on spending the rest of her life either polishing Dr Prole's silver or locked in his asylum, which are the other options open to her. Kiki, too, is so excited at the prospect of returning to the chaotic flat on the sixteenth floor that even the knowledge that "home" includes The Wat Boys doesn't dent his joy.

And all they have to do to go home is get the documents. Easy-peasy, according to some. They know from Constance where Dr Prole used to keep them, in the small study off his library. And, according to Trish, there is no reason to suppose that he didn't put them back there.

"He ain't expecting to have them nicked again, is he?" said Trish. "Not with Constance out of the way." There is, it seems, an advantage to dealing with the terminally arrogant after all.

And so it is that, as the various clocks in the still and darkened house chime two, Trish, with her keychain torch, and Kiki, with his lighted candle stub, tiptoe from Kiki's room. Dr Prole's study is in the other half of the villa, on the ground floor. There are two ways of getting into it: through a door just beyond the front door that leads to the library, and through a door in the pantry that runs through the other half of the cellar to the back stairs. Because Kiki is reluctant to walk through the tombs, the whatnot and the mummy, they take the stairs to the entrance hall.

He stands behind Trish, working his charms and spells, while she silently opens the library door.

"Coo," breathes Kiki. "It's bigger than the one near The Wat."

This is no exaggeration. Dr Prole's library is two storeys high with an encircling, cast-iron walkway where the ceiling should be, the walls all lined with wooden bookcases. Unlike the library near The Wat, Dr Prole's is furnished with comfortable sofas and chairs and tables that exhibit a small but impressive sample of Dr Prole's thousands of artefacts (or knick-knackeries, as Mrs Stump would say).

Trish takes Kiki's hand as they carefully make their soundless way over the carpets and past the displays. "Come on," she whispers. "The study's through that door at the back."

In contrast, the study is small. There is a desk on one side, a fireplace on the other and a walk-through cupboard across from the door that leads to the rear of the house. Next to the door is a large and ancient wooden strongbox, covered in a prayer rug. On top of the rug is a fragment of a carved stone lintel of King Bird Jaguar of Yaxchilan and a large mortar and pestle, also hewn from stone.

The documents, Constance had said, were in the strongbox.

Trish goes straight for the desk. "You get that stuff off the top of the box while I find the key." She opens the lid of the desk, revealing a large writing surface and an array of small compartments, cubbyholes and cubicles. Being a curious sort of girl, Trish can't resist opening a miniature door and pulling out a tiny drawer, just to see what is inside.

"Hurry up!" hisses Kiki. Every creak and groan

of the house sounds to him like Dr Prole or Mrs Stump coming down the stairs. Fear encouraging speed, as it does, he has already cleared the heavy objects from the chest and is lifting off the rug. "I've got a bad feeling."

Trish's fingers search for the trigger at the back that will open the secret compartment where the key to the strongbox is – or was – kept. "You've always got a bad—" With a tiny click the compartment pops open. And in it, just as Constance promised, is the key.

Despite the great age of both, the key turns easily in the strongbox lock.

It is rare, of course, for things to go the way we think they should, but it does happen from time to time.

Kiki stops tapping the roof of his mouth with his tongue. "I don't believe it! They're really there."

And still wrapped in Constance's blue shawl.

"Right." Trish lifts the bulky bundle and puts its on the floor beside her. "Let's get all this back the way it was. He'll never know they're gone."

Trish closes the desk as Kiki puts the mortar and pestle back in place beside King Bird Jaguar.

"Didn't I tell you?" whispers Trish. "Easy-peasy."

Which, unfortunately, turns out to be sadly

optimistic. For at that moment someone starts pounding on the front door as if the hounds of hell are after him.

Kiki and Trish look towards the study door and then back at each other.

"Who could that be?" whispers Trish.

Kiki shakes his head. "I've got a bad feeling."

"Another one?"

"This one's worse," says Kiki.

And is not likely to improve any time soon.

Dr Prole can now be heard, hurrying down the stairs, shouting to Mrs Stump to get back to bed. "I'm coming!" he calls as he reaches the final flight. "For God's sake stop that racket!"

They hear the bolts being pulled back; hear the front door creak open; hear Dr Prole exclaim in mystification and not a small amount of irritation, "Good God, man! Who the deuce are you?"

It is a simple truism, of course, that things can always get worse – but the regularity with which they seem to do so would discourage even a horde of superheroes from ever leaving the house. Now is a good example of what I mean.

"Precisely," comes the reply. "Sir Alistair Deuce, at your service. And, hopefully, you, Dr Prole, are at mine."

Kiki and Trish Eavesdrop on a Very Interesting Conversation

Sir Alistair Deuce has been having quite a time of it lately. Ever since the afternoon Betty Friedman and her cat turned up in the office of the Minister of Housing, he's been rushed off his feet. It has been invigorating in its way – dashing about trying to sort everything out and keep Mr Chumbley from panicking and completely losing his nerve – but it has also been exhausting. And demeaning – especially demeaning. Imagine a member of the aristocracy – a man who, in his time, has helped to raze and plunder more than one great city – running down an old lady like a common joy-rider! And now here he is, back in the malodorous and tiresome past, banging on the door of someone he barely knows – a man whose vision goes no further than his own pocketbook – asking for help like a beggar. It's just as well he has no friends to witness such indignities.

"I apologize for rousing you at such an hour," he says as he follows Dr Prole into his well-apportioned library. "But I can assure you that it is a matter of the utmost importance and urgency."

Dr Prole sets his lamp down and starts to light another, larger lamp on the table beside one of the sofas. "Please, do take a seat." He looks over at his guest, who in many ways is the sort of gentleman he is accustomed to entertaining – wealthy, cosmopolitan and as fashionably turned out as Dr Prole himself (when he isn't in his dressing gown and slippers because he's been banged out of bed in the middle of the night). But there is something in his demeanour – something in those glacial eyes – that sets him apart. That and the facts that he has come unannounced and that his boots aren't polished. "I'm afraid you have me at a bit of a disadvantage, Sir Alistair. You seem to know me, but—"

"And you know me." Sir Alistair gestures to himself. "Though not, of course, as you see me now."

Dr Prole blinks. "Pardon?"

"What I'm about to tell you is in the strictest confidence." Sir Alistair's voice is smooth and almost hypnotically persuasive. "I can't stress enough that I do so only because I find myself in a desperate situation – and because I know you as a kindred spirit whom I can trust." Flattery – no matter how vague – is always a good way of gaining sympathy. As Sir Alistair knows very well.

Taking a seat across from his visitor, Dr Prole nods. "Go on."

Sir Alistair's eyes fix on Dr Prole's like the talons of an owl on a mouse. "To put it as succinctly as possible, I have come from the future." Dr Prole opens his mouth but Sir Alistair doesn't give him the chance to use it. "You must understand that I am not an ordinary mortal like yourself. I am a creature of all realities, capable of moving through time – once I might have been called a druid or a shaman."

"And I, as I'm certain you're aware, am a man of science." If Sir Alistair's smile can curdle milk, Dr Prole's can cool boiling broth. "Do you really expect me to believe that?"

"Yes, yes I do. Science, after all, can only explain so much." Sir Alistair continues to watch his host closely. "And you and I, Erasmus, have discussed the sort of thing I'm talking about on at least one occasion that I can recall. Time travel... Portals..."

It is a testament to how easily impressed Dr Prole is by money and power, two qualities Sir Alistair obviously has in abundance, that this statement doesn't cause him to laugh out loud.

"I'm afraid that—"

"Oh, don't be afraid." Betty Friedman wants to hold on to time, and Sir Alistair wants to obliterate it, but Dr Prole, of course, merely wants to sell it. Knowing this, Sir Alistair changes tack. "I use my gifts to amass my fortunes. And one of the ways I do that is to sell the claptrap of the past to antiquarians and collectors such as yourself." He inclines his head in the doctor's direction. "To you, in fact."

Dr Prole laughs, albeit uneasily. "I don't recall—"

"You don't recall Jacob Jacwyz?" Sir Alistair looks disappointed. "You assault my feelings, Erasmus. We've had so many pleasant dealings – and conversations."

The mention of Jacob Jacwyz makes Dr Prole visibly unsettled. "Are you suggesting that you are—"

"The man who sold you, amongst other things, your priceless mummy – the one that was missing for all those centuries. Surely you must have thought it odd that it should turn up so suddenly after all that time in such pristine condition."

"Anyone might know about my mummy," answers the doctor stiffly.

"Might they also know of the damage to the lid when it was being loaded? Or of those trinkets hidden in the case?"

Trinkets, in this case, meaning the treasures robbed from more than one royal grave.

Dr Prole pales. "Are you trying to blackmail me?"

"And what need would I have for blackmail?" asks Sir Alistair. "What I'm trying to do is get you to help me. I was just about to close a property deal in the twenty-first century that will bring me millions – possibly billions – of pounds."

"Billions?" Dr Prole can hardly imagine such sums.

Sir Alistair nods. "Yes, billions. It's quite staggering how much wealth will be possible in less than one hundred and fifty years from now. I assure you, it's totally mad."

Dr Prole's scepticism gives way to unconcealed interest. Unlike the secrets of the universe, wealth is something he instinctively understands. "And? What happened?"

Sir Alistair shrugs. "There was no opposition, you understand, not for all the tedious months of planning and negotiating and setting it all up – and I certainly wasn't expecting any. But I have an adversary – someone with my talents, but not my philosophy or business sense. Bloody-minded creature's been hounding me almost since the beginning of time. I managed to shake her for a century or two but only a few days ago she suddenly turned up again. Knew all about the property, of course, and is determined to thwart my plans. Once more. Naturally, she wanted to stop the sale. Claimed she had documents that could prove how old and historically important the site is – and what lies beneath it. Fortunately, claiming to have the documents was something of an exaggeration, but she most certainly had an idea where they are."

Dr Prole shakes his head. "I'm afraid I don't see—"

"What this has to do with you?" Sir Alistair raises one eyebrow. "Perhaps if I tell you that the property I'm after is St Barnabas, and I believe that you, my good doctor, may have the documents I seek, it will be clearer."

This information leaves Dr Prole slightly nonplussed, but he manages a rallying smile. "I? But why would you think that I—"

"Because this was dropped by my adversary's accomplices." Sir Alistair removes a photograph from his pocket and leans forward, holding it out towards Dr Prole. "You will note the gentleman standing beside the vicar. I recognized you immediately, of course. Which answered the question of why this nemesis of mine was skulking round the church – and who was most likely to have the documents." He slips the photograph back inside his jacket, but doesn't sit back in his chair. "You do have them, don't you?"

The other man nods. "By chance, yes I do. I'd had my eye on the old strongbox in the vestry for some time, you understand. Not that I knew what was in it, but one never can tell with things like that. That idiot of a vicar knew nothing about it, of course, except that it had been there before the church was built – in the medieval chapel. The key was long gone, which meant there was no way of taking a peek when he wasn't about." So Dr Prole, offering to put a new roof on St Barnabas and redecorate the vicarage, sent the cleric away. He smiles unpleasantly. "Naturally, we couldn't leave the strongbox in the vestry while the work was being done, so I offered to keep it in my museum. For safekeeping."

"Naturally," murmurs Sir Alistair. "That's precisely what I would have done."

Dr Prole's first step, once he had the box, had been to remove the lock and replace it with a similar one to which he did have the key. His second step was to begin to read the documents inside. At which point the work on the roof, which had got no further than putting up the scaffolding, was stopped. There was no sense in repairing the roof when it would be more to his advantage to demolish the church – promising to build a new one –

which would give him the opportunity to secretly excavate the site. "Most of the documents are in a bastardized Latin and difficult hand, which slowed me down quite a bit," explains Dr Prole. "But I understood enough from the outset to appreciate its value." Dr Prole sighs. "I was starting to make my plans when the girl turned up."

"The girl?" If Sir Alistair leans forward any more he will bang his head against Dr Prole's. "What girl?"

"It was the damnedest thing," says Dr Prole. "Came home unexpectedly just a few nights ago and discovered the new maid had been in my things. God knows how she knew about the documents, but she got into the strongbox and made off with them."

Sir Alistair's face darkens like a sky under an approaching storm. "What?"

Understanding only partly the reason for Sir Alistair's concern, Dr Prole says, "Oh it's all right. The boy saw her running through the square as I entered the house. She'd crossed the main road and joined the towpath by the time we caught up, so I went after her on foot. You wouldn't believe how fast she could run."

"Oh no," says Sir Alistair, sinking back into his chair, "no, I believe I would. And I imagine that her destination was St Barnabas itself."

It's possible that, if he spends too much time with Sir Alistair, Dr Prole's uneasy laugh will become permanent. "Why, yes. I finally apprehended her as she was opening the gate. But how—"

"It's simple enough," says Sir Alistair. "I know who this *girl* of yours is."

Dr Prole, though a greedy man, is not a stupid one. "You mean to say that she's— that she's this adversary of yours?"

"In a different incarnation, of course, but otherwise one and the same." Sir Alistair's lips twist sourly. "Obviously, she knew where she'd intended to hide them... But thanks to you she was thwarted." He gives Dr Prole a curt, congratulatory nod. "Dare I ask where she is now?"

Dr Prole always looks smug, but now he looks a little more so. "I assure you, she won't be causing any more trouble in this century. She'll be locked away in my asylum for decades."

"Ah..." Sir Alistair nods. "And that explains why she dropped out of sight for so long. By chance, you did me quite a favour." This is the closest his smile ever comes to pleasure. "But where are the documents now?"

"They're safe." Dr Prole, as Trish and Kiki have been happy to discover, is not a man who believes that lightning strikes the same place twice. "I can assure you of that."

"Well, that is good to hear." Sir Alistair stretches his legs and leans back against the sofa, relieved. "But I'm afraid that I'm going to have to ask you to let me have them."

Dr Prole straightens up. "Let you have them?"

"You know what's under the church," says Sir Alistair. "And you're free to help yourself to what you want." Though well aware of the fact that a new church was never built and the artefacts beneath it never disturbed, Sir Alistair doesn't bring his host's attention to that. "So you really don't have any use for them, do you, Erasmus? Whereas my adversary does have a use for them. And, consequently, so do I. I shan't rest until they're destroyed." Unlike some, Sir Alistair has no qualms about changing what happened in the past.

Dr Prole shakes his head. "Most certainly not. Now that the girl is out of the way, there is no threat to you or your plans that I can see." He smiles tightly, still thinking of Sir Alistair's billions, "Whereas, as I'm sure you appreciate, the documents are quite valuable in themselves. They should be worth a considerable sum to me in time."

Inwardly, Sir Alistair sighs. Though the greedy are easy to manipulate, their inability to see anything more than money can be a nuisance. "I'm afraid you don't understand." Sir Alistair's eyes are darkening again. "My adversary—"

"Don't tell me she's still on the loose."

"Most certainly not." Sir Alistair matches the doctor's slightly mocking tone. "She's back at my hotel."

This news, catching Dr Prole as it does by surprise, causes him to choke. "What?" he gasps. "You brought her with you?"

"What else could I do? I can't let her out of my sight for any length of time. It's too risky. She's wily as they come."

"It's a measure I would only recommend when absolutely necessary, but why don't you simply..." Dr Prole – man of science and medicine, renowned explorer and pillar of society – runs a finger across his own throat.

"That's out of the question." Sir Alistair is very clear on this. "The sooner she dies, the sooner she'll be back."

"In that case, we should put her in my hospital. It's very effective for keeping people out of the way."

"That's impossible." Sir Alistair shakes his head emphatically. "If she is a later incarnation of your girl – which I have no doubt she is – then it would be madness to put them under the same roof, no matter how drugged they're kept."

Dr Prole looks almost amused. "I do think you're unnecessarily concerned. My patients don't know who they are, never mind who anyone else is. And if you're really worried, we can put her in the dungeons – far from where I've got the girl."

"People," intones Sir Alistair. "Your hospital has people – and people are a weak link. Weaker than a tissue. They can be bought, they can be bribed, they can be threatened or cajoled – and they never know when to keep their mouths shut. I want this meddlesome, sentimental old fool put somewhere no one can get at her."

"No one can get at her in the hospital.'

"Perhaps." Sir Alistair gazes at a point over the doctor's shoulder. "But I'm afraid there is another complication."

"Another complication?" It is clear from his tone that Eramus Prole, for one, feels that there have been enough complications to his life already.

"The brats."

"What brats?"

"The children who dropped that photograph. They're involved somehow. And now they've disappeared. Which is one of the reasons it took me so long to find you." Because Kiki Monjate was reported missing by his parents and someone had seen him and Trish near St Barnabas, the police were out in force. Making it impossible for Sir Alistair to get near the Portal until things calmed down. "My chap saw them go into St Barnabas," Sir Alistair continues, "and never saw them come out. Which, if my suspicions are right, means that they're here somewhere – in this century – and they're after the documents. I'm not certain how, though I have my suspicions about that too, but they've got a power they shouldn't have. And so long as they have, they're capable of finding my adversary."

On the other side of the study door, the brats in question look at each other – each thinking of Mrs Calabash – suddenly realizing exactly what power it is that they have.

"But they're just children," argues Erasmus Prole.

"Who vanished." Sir Alistair's lips form a thin, hard line. "Last seen going into the church." He shakes his head. "No, either the documents are destroyed once and for all, or, at the very least, I have to put her somewhere where they can't possibly get to her. At least not until the sale goes through and the new building is begun."

Now Dr Prole's laugh sounds like ice being shaken in a glass container. "What did you have in mind? Antarctica?"

Sir Alistair fails to share his companion's

amusement. "Don't be ridiculous. It would be far too difficult and time-consuming to get her there in this century, and I'm certainly not hauling her back to mine."

Dr Prole looks thoughtful. "Then what about a remote retreat where a very ill old woman could be taken for an indefinite period of isolation and recuperation?"

"You know of a place like that?" Sir Alistair sits up a little straighter. "You mean you will help me?"

"So long as you don't expect me to destroy the documents," says Dr Prole.

"So long as you're certain they're safe."

"I guarantee it."

"And this place?" prompts Sir Alistair. "I take it you have a particular place in mind."

"Indeed I do." Dr Prole nods. "I have a house in the country, extremely remote. The journey would be impossible for your *brats* to undertake."

"But that's excellent." Sir Alistair claps his hands together. "And even if they did manage to get there—"

"Which they won't."

"But if they did, I assume that they wouldn't get within a mile of your house without being seen." Sir Alistair's smile has far less charm than usual. "And taken care of, naturally." He isn't squeamish when it comes to getting rid of children.

"Well..." Dr Prole considers this for a few seconds. "I'm certain it could be arranged. In any event, there is a noon train from King's Cross..."

"Excellent. I—"

"I'll get us a First class compartment. I *insist* on coming with you." Dr Prole can see several advantages to making a friend of Sir Alistair – money not necessarily being the most important. "It's a long and arduous journey. If nothing else, you'll need some company."

Four hands, thinks Sir Alistair, are better than two. "You've persuaded me." He gets to his feet. "Why don't you collect us at eleven? This is my hotel." He takes a card from his pocket and hands it to the doctor. "Oh, and Erasmus, we'll need a carriage that can carry a wheelchair. Bring your medical bag, so you look like a doctor. And a wheelchair, of course."

After Sir Alistair's cab drives off, Dr Prole goes back into the library and opens the study door. The light of his lamp shows only what he expected to see. There are no open drawers in the desk. The strongbox is covered with its rug and artefacts, undisturbed. Dr Prole smiles.

As you'd expect, Trish and Kiki listened to the conversation in the library with unflagging attention. But as soon as it was over, they didn't waste a second vacating the study through the rear entrance. By the time Sir Alistair's cab has gone and Dr Prole has bolted the front door behind him, they have found their way down the back passage and are stepping into the kitchen.

"We've got them! We've got them!" Trish jumps up and down, hugging the shawl against her. "We did, it Kiki! Now we can go home!"

"And what about Betty Friedman?"

Trish stops jumping. In her excitement over being about to SAVE THE DAY at last, Trish had temporarily forgotten about Betty Friedman. "What about her?"

"They're going to stick her in the middle of nowhere in the wrong century, that's what about her. What good are the documents going to do us if we don't have *her*?"

This is such a good point, that Trish doesn't even think of arguing. Emboldened by their success, she says, "Then I reckon we've got to be on that train tomorrow."

"And how are we going to do that?"

"Don't worry," Trish reassures him. "I'll think of something."

Trish Thinks of Something

Mrs Stump, who is very fond of order and doesn't appreciate surprises, is in a high state of agitation the next morning. She simply doesn't know how she's meant to see to everything when people are always changing their plans at the last minute and disrupting her routine.

"Going to the country!" she chants as she thumps round the kitchen. "Well, I never! Going to the country on the spur of the moment, no matter how much there is for me to do."

There is the food to be made for the long journey because Dr Prole says he wants to eat in his compartment, not the dining car. There is Dr Prole's case to be packed as he has had to rush off to the hospital for something. There is the telegram to be sent ahead to make certain the house is in order. There is getting Trish and Kiki to the station by eleven-thirty with Dr Prole's things.

Mrs Stump, unknowingly coming to Trish and Kiki's assistance, insists that Trish accompany Kiki to the train in the event that there aren't any porters available and someone is needed to mind the carriage while Kiki fills that job. Dr Prole is far too great and important a man to carry his own luggage.

"If he misses his train it'll come out of your hide, my boy," she assures Kiki. "Out of your hide. And there's not much of that going spare, is there?"

Because of Mrs Stump's agitated state and the general frenzy of preparations, it isn't until Dr Prole's portmanteau and the wicker hamper of provisions have been loaded onto the landau and they set off for the station that Trish has the chance to announce her plan for rescuing Betty Friedman.

"Didn't I say I'd think of something?" she crows. "And it's so simple it can't possibly go wrong. We're going to be back home in no time."

Kiki glances over at her. "Really?"

"Really." Pretty pleased with her own cleverness, Trish laughs. "All we have do is get on the train and then we grab Betty Friedman and get off at the next stop."

It is only because Kiki believes that Mrs Stump sending Trish to the station with him is a positive sign from the powers of the cosmos that he doesn't laugh out loud. "What, just take her right out from under their noses? Us and what army?"

"Dr Prole and Sir Kiss-My-Bum have to leave their compartment sometime," reasons Trish. "You know, to use the loo or whatever."

Kiki shakes his head. "They're keeping an eye on her, remember? You heard what Sir Alistair said. She's well wily. If they're eating in their compartment, they're not going to go to the toilet together."

"Well that's all right." Trish holds the lidded shopping basket that contains the precious bundle of documents with one hand and clamps her other hand on the side of the seat a bit harder so as not to bounce out of the carriage. "Divide and conquer, right? As soon as one of them leaves the compartment, we can distract the other one."

"And how will we do that?"

"I'll think of something," says Trish.

Kiki shakes his head again. "I don't know... I think it's well dodgy getting stuck on a train with those two." It is difficult to do a runner from a moving train.

"But we've got to get on the train," moans Trish. "You're the one who said we've got to rescue her. Well, we can't rescue her if she's in the country and we're in London, can we?"

Kiki drives slowly, keeping his eyes on the road, trying to avoid hitting the many people, animals and holes in the ground that constantly get in their way.

"Yeah, but, it's not going to work. Even if we can get Betty Friedman away from them, they're going to notice pretty quick that she's gone. And then they'll come looking for her." Kiki knows there are few places, if any, to hide on a train. "What are we going to do when they catch up with us?"

"You worry too much. We just have to get on the train, then everything will sort itself out." Trish looks down at their feet. "We've got Mrs Calabash, ain't we? And Mrs Calabash is the power."

"And what's she going to do? I mean, I know she's some sort of power, but she wasn't enough to stop Betty Friedman getting kidnapped, was she?"

Trish gives him a scornful look. "Are you being thick on purpose or what? Of course she didn't stop Sir Kiss-My-Bum. She wasn't *with* Betty Friedman then, was she? She was with us." Like many people who come late to an idea, Trish is now such a firm believer in Mrs Calabash's magical abilities that there is no room for doubt.

"Trish—" It is unclear to him how it happened, but Kiki now seems to be the voice of logic and

254

reason. "Trish, you have to have a real plan. You know, one where everything is worked out."

"I've told you my plan! We get on the train—"

"And how do we do that without any money?"

"I'll think of something."

"You know what your problem is?" Kiki doesn't wait for her to ask to be enlightened on this matter. "Your problem is you don't worry enough. You don't think things through. You just act."

Trish sits up very stiff and straight with indignation. "And you know what your trouble is? You think too much. It's always 'what if that happens?' and 'what if this happens?' Maybe if you just got on with things instead of crossing your fingers and tapping your toes we wouldn't be in this mess now."

"*Me?*"

"Yes, you! If you'd sorted out The Wat Boys 'stead of trying to avoid them, none of this would've happened."

Kiki is sitting up pretty stiff and straight himself now. "And if you hadn't dragged me into the cottage none of this would've happened either."

"That's right," snaps Trish. "It would've been you in hospital and me at home watching telly and eating chips." She points to a large ornate building rising above the shops and houses. "Look, there it is!"

"All I'm saying is that you don't work out what could happen. You overlook things." Kiki turns into the carriageway in front of the station.

"Oh, I do, do I?" Trish raises her chin. "And what things have I overlooked this time?"

As it happens, one of the things that Trish has overlooked is now in plain view. Just inside the main entrance, standing with his back to them. Next to him is Dr Prole and an unidentifiable figure bundled up in a dark blanket and slumped in a wheelchair.

"What about *him*?" Kiki nods to the overlooked thing. "What if Sir Alistair twigs that it's us?"

"Don't be daft," says Trish. "He ain't never seen us, has he? And even if he did, he wouldn't recognize us in this gear, would he?"

"Yes he would. He's looking for two kids, remember? And if the police were out looking for us, he may have seen our pictures on the telly." As they come to a stop, Dr Prole takes a gold watch from his pocket, checks the time, and looks impatiently towards the entrance. Seeing his carriage, he turns back to his companion. Despite the fact that Trish and Kiki are too far away to hear what they're saying, it is obvious that Dr Prole is going to go ahead with the wheelchair, and that Sir Alistair is coming to the carriage to see to the

256

bags. Kiki groans. "What'd I tell you? He's coming over!"

One of the advantages of not working things out beforehand is that you learn to think on your feet. While Kiki is transfixed, not to say paralysed, by the sight of Sir Alistair Deuce descending upon them, Trish is scanning the entrance and the people milling about for somewhere to hide. Her eyes fall on a large and rather startling looking man in a wide-brimmed black hat and long black cape who stands at the centre of a chaotic group disembarking from Hackney carriages behind them. Stickers on the trunks being hurled to the ground announce that they are *The Padua Players – England's Premier Troop of Travelling Actors.* The more genteel folk around them seem to view the actors as the rabble and scum Mrs Stump described and are darting dark, wary looks their way and keeping their distance, but what Trish sees is salvation.

"I'll disappear," says Trish, jumping out of the landau with her basket. "He won't be suspicious if you're on your own." She holds out her arms. "Give me Mrs Calabash."

Kiki obediently lifts Mrs Calabash from between his feet and hands her down to Trish so carefully that she doesn't even wake. "But wh—"

Trish, however, has already melted into the

257

noisy throng that is The Padua Players. It is from this vantage point that she watches Sir Alistair hail a porter and then stroll across the station to Dr Prole's gleaming black carriage with its fine gold trim and red leather seats.

Kiki pulls his cap over his eyes, and begins chanting to himself and tapping the roof of his mouth, which at least dulls the sound of the pounding of his heart as he peers under the brim to watch Sir Alistair approaching with a porter.

Fortunately, Kiki's fear of being discovered proves to be exaggerated, as much fear is, of course. Like Dr Prole, Sir Alistair's manner of dealing with servants is to give orders, make complaints and otherwise ignore them so completely that they might not be there. He barely glances at Kiki as he barks, "Help the porter load the bags, boy, and then you may go. Tell Mrs Stump that Dr Prole shall send word when he's ready to return."

"Yes, sir," mumbles Kiki, and jumps down to unstrap the case and the hamper and load them onto the porter's trolley. Sir Alistair stands to one side, shouting, "Careful!" and "Watch it!" – and all the while Kiki hardly breathes lest he catches his attention. It isn't until Sir Alistair finally saunters into the station, the porter following behind, that Kiki collapses joyously against the landau, and starts breathing regularly again. At least that's over.

But Kiki himself has overlooked the fact that when one thing ends another usually begins. Sir Alistair is still visible inside the terminal, heading to his platform, when Trish and Mrs Calabash reappear at Kiki's side.

"Come on." Trish tugs at his arm. "Let's go."

"Go?" Kiki repeats. "Go where?"

"To Switzerland, where do you think?" Seeing that Kiki is about to repeat her words again, Trish says, "Crikey ... to the blinkin' train. Now hurry."

Kiki has no intention of hurrying anywhere, but Trish has hold of his arm and pulls him along with her as if he were a balloon.

"But we can't leave the carriage..." protests Kiki. "And we don't have any money..."

Trish grins. "Didn't I tell you I'd think of something?" She jerks her head towards The Padua Players, who, in their boisterous and undisciplined way, are also making their way towards the platforms. "That's why we're following them, isn't it? I heard them say they're taking the noon train."

"And what good does that do us?" gasps Kiki, as she drags him along. "We can't get on that train, Trish, we don't have tickets."

"But that's the point, we *can* get on the train. With *them*. No one's going to notice if they've got a couple of extra kids with them. Just stay close and walk through like we're part of the group. I've seen it done hundreds of times."

This is true, but Trish fails to take into consideration that the places she's seen this trick done have all been on television. Getting past the guard at the gate proves slightly more difficult than it is on screen.

Mr Jupiter Padua, manager and male lead of The Padua Players, shows his clutch of tickets to the guard and stands aside to let his troop pass onto the steam-clouded platform. Flicking his cape over his shoulder, he starts after them just as Trish and Kiki finally reach the gate. Kiki closes his eyes as he and Trish sail past the guard, but they have only gone a few paces when a hand falls on each of their shoulders in a very persuasive way.

"Just a minute, you two. Let's see your tickets."

"But you've seen our tickets. We're with them," blusters Trish, trying to squirm free from the grasp of the guard. "We're with The Padua Players!"

Hearing his name, Jupiter Padua also stops, and turns round. "Pardon?"

The ground not having opened and swallowed him whole, it's all Kiki can do not to faint on the spot.

"These two with you?" calls the guard, giving them a shake.

Jupiter Padua can't look right into Kiki's eyes, since they are shut, but he can look right into Trish's. Knowing that she has nothing to lose, Trish stares back boldly, mouthing the word *Please*.

Being an actor, Jupiter Padua has both a flexible nature and a marked quickness of wit. He is also not one to miss a dramatic moment, and throws back his head and cries in a voice that would reach the farthest corner of the largest theatre in the world, "Good God, man! Unhand those children. Of course they're with me!" in a way that makes further questions impossible. Jupiter Padua may not be a truly great actor, but he is a very kind man.

"Well, keep 'em with you in future," grumbles the guard, as he releases Trish and Kiki and shoves them forward none too gracefully.

"I do think you two owe me an explanation," says Jupiter Padua as the three of them hurry to catch up with the others.

Kiki gives Trish a look. "Should we tell him the truth?" he whispers.

Trish doesn't think so. Trish thinks that the truth is far too complicated, not to mention improbable, to be of much use in this situation. "That's the last thing we want to tell him," she whispers back.

"And what's the first?"

"Don't worry," says Trish. "I'll think of something."

"I thought you'd already done that," says Kiki.

They May Not Be Angels but They Talk as if They Are Gods

In the first-class carriage of the noon train, Dr Erasmus Prole and Sir Alistair Deuce lean back against the forward-facing seats of their comfortably appointed compartment. The opposite seats are occupied by Dr Prole's "very ill" (and very drugged) patient, Elizabeth Martha Friedman. Betty Friedman sleeps; Dr Prole and Sir Alistair are deep in conversation. Betty Friedman's sleep is deep and dreamless. The gentlemen's conversation is animated and warm. The life of a Time Keeper, even a Renegade Time Keeper, can be lonely. Time Keepers don't have conferences or meetings or conventions or belong to a club. They may from time to time hear of someone or something that makes them smile inwardly and think, *ah, a comrade, a kindred soul,* or perhaps *yes, I know what that's about;* from time to time their paths may even cross – but they very rarely meet. Time

Keepers don't normally have friends.

But Sir Alistair now has a companion – and an audience.

As the train steams out of the terminus and into the nearby countryside, Sir Alistair points out all the things that will no longer be there in the coming centuries with considerable delight. *Those fields will all be gone... Those woods... That farm... That village... Concrete as far as the eye can see... Endless motorways and shopping centres and superstores...* And then, of course, has to interrupt himself to explain what motorways and shopping centres and superstores are.

Dr Prole's feelings as he listens are evenly divided between awe and amazement. "I like to think that I have vision," he says when he can finally squeeze a word in. "And I have more imagination than most – but what you describe is—"

"Beyond belief, I know." Sir Alistair smiles proudly, as someone who has done his bit to help these things along might be expected to. "Ah, the future, Erasmus ... the future!" enthuses Sir Alistair. "You can't imagine such staggering wealth... Such ingenious technology..." He might add, *Such indecent luxury... Such extraordinary self-indulgence... Such heart-warming devastation*, but doesn't in case the doctor is more sentimental than he seems. "And it's men such as yourself who have made it all possible..."

But Dr Prole is less interested in his own contribution to the future than he is in the future itself. "Even with the glorious empires of the past and present as inspiration, it hardly seems credible." He gives Sir Alistair a coaxing smile. "Are you certain you're not exaggerating just the tiniest bit?"

"Exaggerating?" Sir Alistair smirks. "Not in the slightest. If anything, I'm being restrained. Let me tell you about wealth, my friend. There are men in my time who could spend your entire fortune on lunch." He slaps his thigh. "On lunch, Erasmus! Five times your fortune on a watch! A watch – when only a short while ago people told the time by the sun! How inspiring is that? And would you like to hear the best part?"

A new feeling has joined awe and amazement in what passes for Dr Prole's heart, and that is envy. "Yes," he says with sincerity. "I would indeed."

"It is no longer kings or governments that run the world, Erasmus, it's men like you and me! Entrepreneurs! Businessmen! Men who embrace the future and know how to turn a profit from the past."

Dr Prole would like to do more than embrace the future – he would like to set up shop in it. "It sounds as if I was born in the wrong century," he says, with a mirthless laugh.

"And what progress, my good doctor!" Sir Alistair goes on. "Fantastic, unsentimental, determined progress that makes this pitiful century look no better than the Stone Age. You think this train is something? You think this is fast?" He laughs. "We have planes, Erasmus. Machines that fly in the sky like birds. You can travel the world in a matter of hours, you can cross this entire nation in a matter of minutes." He refills his glass from one of the bottles of wine thoughtfully provided by Mrs Stump. "And the cities! X'ian, Mohenjo-daro, Cuzco and Helike were never more than outposts next to them. Thebes, Athens, Rome and Constantinople no more than villages. Now we have towering cities of glass and steel."

"But what about the cities of today? London... Paris... Dresden...?"

"Oh, some of the old ones still stand, or parts of them do – like the Pyramids and just about as useful – but they've been built up and built over and added onto. Their days are numbered." Sir Alistair looks like he may purr. "But it's in destruction that mankind has really surpassed itself. Tanks... machine guns... missiles... grenades... fantastic bombs dropped from the sky that can level a city... You can't begin to imagine the profits in things like that, Erasmus! It boggles even my mind – billions and billions and billions of pounds!"

Dr Prole is trying very hard to begin to imagine the profits. Indeed, he is far more successful than Sir Alistair would have supposed, for he can actually see himself raking them in. "There is one question I wanted to ask you," he murmurs.

"Yes?"

This time it is Dr Prole who refills Sir Alistair's glass. "I wanted to ask you about Time Portals."

They May not Be Gods but They Could Be Angels

Trish and Kiki are not what one might call seasoned rail travellers. Kiki has been once on the overground to Richmond Park on a family outing, and Trish took the train to Hastings with her mother for a day at the seaside that failed to live up to expectations (as many of the ex-Mrs O'Leary's days do). Needless to say, neither of these experiences has prepared them for the unadorned Third Class, nineteenth-century carriage they now find themselves in.

"Sit down! Sit down!" booms Jupiter Padua. "Make yourselves comfortable."

This is impossible, of course. The only way they could be more uncomfortable would be if the hard, wooden seats were being dragged over the tracks behind the train.

"I'll never complain about the 36 bus again," mutters Kiki as the train gets underway. They are so near the wheels and the engine that they might as well be in a wagon riding over rocks in a dust storm.

Pressed between Jupiter Padua and Kiki, like jam between two pieces of bread, Trish says, "I'll never complain about anything again."

The Padua Players, however, are accustomed to crowded trains and cramped rooms, and settle in with admirable ease, chatting and laughing as they remove packets of sandwiches and pieces of fruit from their bags and share them out amongst the troop.

They also share their stories. Always happy to find themselves with a new audience, the actors are soon competing with each other to tell the funniest or most outrageous account of their considerable travels round the country, most of which seem to feature untrustworthy theatre managers, ungrateful theatre-goers and narrow escapes from one disaster or another.

"Remember the time they ran us out of Newcastle?" one tale will start, and the next will begin with, "That's nothing compared to when we had to leave that hotel in Bristol in the dead of night."

Unlike Dr Prole, who is dedicated to acquisition, and Mrs Stump, who is dedicated to complaining, the Padua Players are dedicated to living, and soon Kiki and Trish are laughing so much that they no longer notice their numb bottoms or feet, or the layer of soot that has seeped in through the windows. Indeed, they are enjoying themselves so much that they are a bit taken aback when Jupiter Padua, despite the small space and his rather large size, rises to his feet and claps his hands for silence.

"And now," he announces, "our new friends have a story of their own to tell." He bows to Trish, knocking the hat off the head of the woman behind him. "M'lady, if you would be so kind…"

"Well…" Trish looks round at the eager and expectant faces.

"Come, come!" chides Jupiter Padua. "Your audience is waiting, and one must never keep an audience waiting."

"Or they'll rip out the seats and throw them at the stage!" calls someone at the back.

"Enough! Enough!" Jupiter Padua beats down the laughter with a wave of his hands. "I, for one, am exceedingly anxious to discover why you compromised my good name by getting me to lie for you," he says to Trish, though not unkindly. "An explanation is very much in order."

"Don't be shy, ducky," says the woman who had her hat knocked off. "You're amongst friends, you know. There's not one of us hasn't had to adjust the truth from time to time."

"Or simply give it a decent burial," laughs the woman beside her.

Trish nods and smiles (which in this instance is her equivalent of crossing her fingers and tapping her tongue against the roof of her mouth). Since they are actors, she reckons that her explanation should be gripping and dramatic; and since they are generous and good-natured enough to help total strangers it should also be something that will tug at the sensitive strings of their hearts.

"Well..." she says again. "You see, it was like this... My dear old gran – Nana Friedman – she's the gentlest and sweetest old dear you could ever hope to meet. She'd give you her last piece of chocolate, that's how kind she is."

There is an appreciative chorus of "oohs" and "aahs" from The Padua Players.

Encouraged, Trish gets into her tale. "And she's always been so good to me. Always looking out for me and worrying about me." She looks over at Kiki. "And to him, too. Ain't she, Kiki? Ain't she always been so good to you?" His eyes on his knees, Kiki nods. "Anyway," Trish continues, "Nana Friedman's got this nephew. From the other side of the family. He's a lord and all, but my mum says that Alistair – that's his name – my mum says that Alistair couldn't be more evil if his dad was the devil himself. He's really cruel and mean, like he'd take your last biscuit from you if you was starving, just to see you suffer. That's the sort of bloke he is."

"What a scoundrel," says the woman whose hat was knocked off.

"That's right," agrees Trish. "He's a right scoundrel."

The other Padua Players contribute another round of "oohs" and "aahs".

"So anyway," Trish continues, "Alistair squandered his fortune and now he owes all this money to the gambling syndicate and drug dealers and people like that." She isn't herself entirely certain what a gambling syndicate is, but, fortunately, no one asks for a definition. "He wanted gran to give him the money he owes, but she said she won't help him out of trouble any more. You know, because she's done it so many times before."

"He's made his bed so he's got to lie in it!" chips in a man across the aisle. Several people agree.

"So you know what he did?" Trish's eyes are wide. "He kidnapped her! That's what he did. He's got her on this train, and he going to hold her prisoner in his castle in the middle of nowhere until she makes out a will in his favour, and then he's going to kill her and dump her body in the moat where no one'll find it for hundreds of years." Trish ends this tragic story of greed and betrayal with a breathless flourish. "So you see, that's why we had to get on the train. It's a matter of life and death." If there were a bit more room she'd be wringing her hands.

Jupiter Padua, who has been listening with the rapt attention audiences often give to his performances, applauds. "That's quite a story." He turns to the members of his troupe. "Don't you agree? Indeed, if I'm not mistaken, I believe we did a play with a similar plot only last season." He cocks his head to one side and smiles at Trish. "But, as fond as I am of fiction, my dear, I think that this time we would all very much prefer the truth."

Kiki, who has been listening to Trish with the rapt attention of someone who can't believe his own ears, would very much prefer the truth as well. Kiki reasons that although The Padua Players are not movie stars (and, therefore, not gods), they are actors – which could be almost as helpful. Actors, Kiki, knows, have both imagination and a fondness for the past (or at least for old plays), which means that they might be sympathetic to what is really going on.

And so, before Trish can protest that she *is* telling the truth, Kiki says, "Well, to start with, me and Trish come from the future. From the twenty-first century."

This is the sort of announcement that might be expected to get a laugh or even hoots of derision from most people, but The Padua Players simply nod as though they knew it all along.

"Now, *that's* what I call a very good beginning," says Jupiter Padua.

It turns out to be a very good middle and ending, too; one that holds his audience spellbound.

"So that's why we asked you to lie so we could get on the train," Kiki finishes. "We've got to save Betty Friedman and keep Sir Alistair from turning the church into a block of flats."

Everyone starts talking at once. About being run over and being ignored by the law. About travelling through time and the aristocracy. About the importance of history and respecting the past. About Kiki and Trish's bravery. Even about Dr Prole. "He'd take the Good Lord off the cross to sell the nails, if he could," says one of The Padua Players, and the others all tut and nod.

"And that creature there—" Jupiter Padua points to Mrs Calabash, sleeping on Kiki's lap. "Would that be your friend Betty Friedman's catawampus, perhaps?"

"She's a cat," says Trish.

"That, too." Mr Padua smiles. "But from what your young friend has been saying I'd wager she's your good woman's familiar as well."

"Betty Friedman's not a witch," says Kiki staunchly. "She's a Time Keeper. That's different."

"Indeed it is," agrees the manager and chief male actor of The Padua Players. "Indeed it is." He looks to his troupe. "The Bard was right again!" he cries. "'There are more things in Heaven and Earth, Horatio, than are dreamt of in your philosophy...'"

Trish looks from Jupiter Padua and his players to Kiki and back again. "You mean you believe him?"

"Of course we believe him. Unlike *your* story, young lady, your friend's is both too original and too improbable not to be true." Jupiter Padua puts his fingertips together, his expression thoughtful. "The question now, of course, is how we are going to help you free your Betty Friedman. Obviously, we daren't try to take her by force."

"Why not?" asks Trish. It works on the telly.

"Because, my dear child, Dr Prole is a man of great wealth and renown – a very special guest at the banquet of life. While we, alas, are but poor beggars standing at the kitchen door in the rain with our caps in our hands, asking for crumbs."

"What's that mean?" asks Kiki.

"It means that if we laid a finger on him or his friend we'd find ourselves performing behind bars or dangling from a gibbet, that's what it means. I have no intention of hanging from a gibbet, if it's all the same to you." He screws up his mouth and furrows his brow. "No ... we need something cunning ... something clever ... something—" He breaks off, slapping his thigh so hard that everyone round him jumps. "By Jove! I swear, I'm as blind as Lear! The play's the thing, is it not?"

"The play?" repeat Trish and Kiki.

Jupiter Padua raises his eyes to the heavens, which in this case is the ceiling of the Third Class carriage. "Yes!" he booms. "The play!"

Trish looks over at Kiki and grins. "Didn't I tell you everything'd work out?"

Jupiter Padua Gives the Performance of a Lifetime – and Trish and Kiki Don't Do Badly, Either

Having found an empty compartment where the second act of the afternoon's drama is to be played, Jupiter Padua is ready to begin Act One. He stands in front of Dr Prole and Sir Alistair's door, preparing himself for what may very well be one of his greatest performances. He has exchanged his wide-brimmed hat and cape for a frock coat and top hat, and added a monocle to reinforce the image of what Mrs Stump, amongst others, would call a proper gentleman. Being a large man with the sort of thin, fleshless features often considered aristocratic (as though Nature's lack of generosity is an indication of quality), the effect is quite impressive – as long as you don't notice the holes in his boots.

Curtain up! – Jupiter Padua says to himself. He raises his hand and raps firmly on the door like a man who is accustomed to being greeted with polite words and smiles wherever he goes (which, sadly, is not the case).

Almost immediately the door is opened by none other than the eminent Dr Erasmus Prole himself, filling the space in such a way that it is impossible to get even a small glimpse inside the compartment.

"Yes?" This word is said with moderate politeness, but without any trace of a smile – though an eyebrow does twitch in surprise. Dr Prole was expecting the steward with tea. "May I help you?"

Acting as though he has been warmly greeted, Jupiter Padua extends his hand, now adorned with several rings that can pass for gold as long as one doesn't actually bite them. "I am Sir Bartimus Pearce," he says. "Perhaps you have heard of me?"

"No." Dr Prole does not give the impression that he considers this any sort of loss. "No, I haven't."

Jupiter Padua smiles. "Ah … but I, of course, have heard of you. Dr Erasmus Prole, is it not? Naturally, I recognize your face from the papers."

"Pardon me…" Dr Prole still shows no sign of being able to smile himself. "But how did you—"

"Know that you're here?" Jupiter Padua clasps his hands. "I do hope you won't take offence, but your reputation goes before you like the Royal

Guard before the Queen, Dr Prole." Jupiter smiles bashfully. "And I'm afraid that the conductor told me you are on board. He took pity on me, you see." What the conductor actually took was the price of a beer. "He seemed certain that you might help me."

"Did he?" But Erasmus Prole, not unusually, as we know, is softened by the flattery. He gives a gracious nod. "And how may I be of service?"

"I really am terribly sorry to disturb you," Jupiter Padua apologizes. "And I assure you that I wouldn't trouble you like this if it weren't a matter of some urgency." He wrings his hands in a well-bred but anguished way. "The things is that I am travelling with my daughter, Lady Jane Cahill-Smith... You may be acquainted with her husband – quite a collector of antiquities, like yourself, though not in your league, of course. The sad fact is that my dear child has been taken very ill all of a sudden. She is in the greatest discomfort and distress. We've done everything that we can – her mother and I – but she seems to worsen by the minute. And, though I have searched, there doesn't seem to be another doctor on the train ... and so I was hoping... If I could claim a few minutes of your valuable time... I am afraid it may be something serious... Our compartment's just in the next carriage..."

As Jupiter Padua knows, powerful, wealthy and important men like Dr Prole are almost as fond of titles as they are of flattery.

"Why, certainly... Of course... Lady Cahill-Smith, you say? You know, I do believe I have come across her husband. I may even have sold him some Roman trinket... Fortunately, I have my bag with me. Just wait there one second while I fetch it." He slips back inside, firmly shutting the door.

Jupiter Padua glances to the end of the car, where Kiki, Trish, Mrs Calabash and two of the younger actors who double as stagehands are watching the play from the wings, which in this case means behind the door of the observation deck. He gives them a conspiratorial wink, then turns round quickly as the door opens again.

A few minutes after Jupiter has led the esteemed doctor into the next carriage, an elderly woman appears in the corridor. She wears a large hat and walks none too steadily with a cane. This is, in fact, Rosie Threadle, whose Lady Macbeth made The Padua Players such a hit on the south coast the summer before. As she nears Dr Prole and Sir Alistair's compartment she begins to cry – not loudly enough to wake the dead, perhaps, but loudly enough to disturb the peace and quiet of Sir Alistair Deuce.

Once more the door of the compartment opens. Since Sir Alistair is fairly certain that it isn't the steward with the tea (the stewards of First Class carriages have never been known to weep while on duty), he feels no need to be even moderately polite. "What in damnation's going on?" he demands.

In answer, Rose Threadle collapses against him, wailing and sobbing uncontrollably.

Kiki and Trish (and Mrs Calabash) duck back below the window and the two actors turn to face the receding landscape. But although none of them can see what is happening they can hear it perfectly well.

The old woman refuses to be got rid of. She is, as she tearfully explains, half-blind (and in Sir Alistair's opinion half-witted as well), and has lost her way coming from the dining car and can't find her compartment.

"For God's sake, woman!" shouts Sir Alistair. "Stop wailing like a banshee and we'll find your blasted seat for you. It isn't that big a train."

The door shuts again (very loudly) and the voices – the old woman's crying and Sir Alistair's (in the genteel way of the upper class) ordering her to put a sock in it or find herself left in the baggage car – move slowly away.

When the corridor is silent once more, Trish and

Kiki and Mrs Calabash cautiously raise their faces to the window of the observation deck as the actors, equally cautiously, turn around. Mrs Calabash starts to do her impersonation of a hovering helicopter.

Trish takes a deep breath. "I reckon that's our cue," she whispers, though whether she means the empty corridor or the sounds coming from Mrs Calabash is hard to say.

"We'll wait here," says one of the actors. "Just give a shout if you need us."

Kiki leaves the door to the observation deck slightly ajar as he and Trish tiptoe into the corridor. Mrs Calabash continues to hum and rattle, but Kiki and Trish barely dare breathe as they open Dr Prole and Sir Alistair's compartment and quickly slip inside.

Betty Friedman is stretched out on one of the plush seats, covered by a dark blanket, her eyes shut tight.

This, of course, is one part of the play that couldn't be scripted.

"Betty!" Trish rushes over to her. "Betty!" Trish puts her head to the old woman's chest, and is relieved to hear a heartbeat. "Betty!" Trish cries in her ear. "Betty! You've got to wake up!"

If she doesn't wake up, they will have to call the actors to carry her out to the observation desk –

and pray that she isn't found before the train makes a stop and they can get her safely off.

"Betty!" calls Kiki. "Betty, Mrs Calabash is here. She's really missed you."

Trish gives the motionless figure a gentle shake. "Miss Friedman! Please, you've got to wake up right now! There isn't much time."

But Betty Friedman still doesn't move. It is now that Mrs Calabash, who has missed her owner very much indeed, takes matters into her own paws as it were, and leaps from Kiki's arms to the figure on the seat, rubbing against the old woman, and sounding very much as though she's about to blow them all up like one of the bombs Sir Alistair so admires.

Trish continues to plead. "Betty! Betty! Please wake up!"

Betty Friedman's eyes open slowly, one hand reaching up to rest on Mrs Calabash's head. "Do stop shrieking in my ear like that, Trish O'Leary," she orders. "I've been drugged, not murdered."

"Oh, Betty!" Trish is so relieved that she nearly sobs. "You're alive!"

Betty Friedman pulls herself up to a sitting position, lifting Mrs Calabash onto her lap as she does so. "Of course I'm alive." She looks round for the first time. "But where on earth are we?"

"We're on a train," says Kiki.

"I can see that," snaps Betty Friedman. "And at a guess I'd say it's a train in the nineteenth century. Latter half, if I'm not mistaken."

"We don't have time for this," cuts in Trish. "We've got to get out of here before Dr Prole and Sir Alistair come back."

"Dr Prole?" Betty Friedman smiles. "Well, isn't Alistair clever to have found Erasmus. Sometimes I think I don't give him nearly enough credit."

"They're working together," says Kiki. "It was Sir Alistair's idea to take you somewhere Trish and I would never find you. That's why we're on a train."

"And sometimes I think I give him too much credit." Careful not to disturb Mrs Calabash, Betty Friedman slides her legs over the edge of the seat, moving her feet as though testing to see that they still work. "Or perhaps he doesn't give me enough."

Trish moves to the door, debating whether or not to lock Dr Prole and Sir Alistair out – which would, obviously, have the effect of locking the four of them in. While she's confident that the two young men lurking on the observation deck could easily carry Betty Friedman, she isn't as certain that they could take on Dr Prole and a Renegade Time Keeper. "The important thing is that we get out of here!" she repeats.

Betty Friedman turns to look at the green, green hills of the English countryside moving by. "My, my, how pretty it was."

Kiki and Trish haven't had much time to gaze out the window since they boarded the train, but now the tone of regret in Betty Friedman's voice makes them do just that. It is more than pretty. With no motorways, or housing developments or pylons or shopping centres or planes to mar the view it has a depth that almost seems like a tunnel back through the memories of time.

Betty Friedman sighs. "I presume that we're on our way to one of Dr Prole's country retreats."

"That's right," says Trish, coming quickly back to the moment they're in. "But we've really got to—"

Betty Friedman continues to gaze out the window. "Well, will you look where we are..."

Trish and Kiki both look.

"We're not nowhere," grumbles Trish.

"It's just fields and hills," adds Kiki.

Betty Friedman adjusts Mrs Calabash over her neck like a shawl and gets to her feet. "To you it may be nowhere and just fields and hills, but to me it is our way back home. Where, if you'll recall, we have a very important meeting to attend." As if she already knows the answer to the question she's about to ask, she looks at Trish.

"Do you have the documents?"

Trish holds up the lidded basket. "Yeah, only we really have to get out of here—"

"But of course we do." Betty Friedman pulls down the window on the outside door of the compartment, reaches her hand through it, and opens the door. "That's why we're getting off here, isn't it?"

Trish wonders if, despite Mrs Calabash's considerable power, Betty Friedman has actually recovered from the drugs she's been given. "Are you mad?"

"Most certainly not."

"But we can't just walk out of a moving train," protests Kiki.

"Of course we can," says Betty Friedman. And before they can stop her, she takes each of them firmly by a hand and steps into the nothing-but-fields-and-hills of the beautiful English countryside.

By now (although they are certainly not unmoved by the experience) neither Trish nor Kiki can be said to be truly astonished to discover that not only are they not dead, but that they are walking.

"I believe that what we are looking for is just over this hill," Betty Friedman announces as she marches them upwards through the high grass.

Thinking that Betty Friedman must have a very

fast car, a small plane or even a magic carpet or an especially large broomstick waiting for them just over the hill, Kiki and Trish scrabble up the rocky slope as quickly as they can.

"There we are!" cries Betty Freedman as they gain the crest. "What did I tell you?"

In front of them is a circle of very large, old stones.

Trish makes no attempt to hide her dismay. "It's rocks. How are we going to get home on a bunch of rocks?"

Kiki, however, is shaking his head. He has seen this sort of thing before – if on a much smaller scale. "No, it's not just a bunch of rocks. It's some sort of shrine."

"It is heartening to see that one of you has some sense of the past," says Betty Friedman. "Those rocks happen to be sacred standing stones."

"And?" Trish is not impressed. "They don't look like they're standing very well to me."

"And you'll do as I say," says Betty Friedman. "I'm not about to give you a crash course in the workings of the cosmos right now. That will have to wait for a later date."

"Oh, please," says an all-too-familiar voice directly behind then. "There's no need for you to hurry. It's a long time since I've heard you do your 'the stories told under starry skies … dreams born in a sunrise...' routine. All that mystical rubbish you've been spouting through the millennia. I'd truly love to hear what you have to say to the child."

Sir Alistair Deuce is standing a metre or two away, swinging an ebony walking stick as though merely out for a pleasant stroll. "And, please, don't leave out any of your sentimental claptrap about the oneness of the universe and the time continuum and the importance of cosmic memories, my dear Azi—" His smile is blacker than his cane. "Oh, but that's not right, is it? What is it this incarnation – for the life of me, I can't seem to keep it in my head." He frowns. "Belinda? Bathsheba?" He taps the stick against the ground. "Oh, I know! It's Betty, isn't it? Petty Betty, all a twitter because a few old buildings get knocked down and people don't paint themselves blue and dance in the moonlight any more."

Betty Friedman doesn't seem at all surprised to see him. "One almost has to admire your persistence," she says. "It's such a pity you can't put it to some good purpose. You did have such great promise in the old days."

He gives her one of his this-will-freeze-hell-over smiles. "And I, of course, might say the same about you. But the dreams of youth do so often go belly up, don't they?" He steps towards them, pointing the cane at Betty Friedman.

Trish and Kiki automatically move closer to her.

"Let's not play any more games. I'm going to take a wild guess that my documents are in that very fetching basket the young lady is holding. Why don't we start by handing it over to me?"

Trish tightens her grip on the handle of the basket and moves so close to Betty Friedman that she is nearly on top of her.

Sir Alistair takes another step, pointing his cane now at Kiki and Trish. "I'm sure your friend *Betty* realizes, even if you don't, that you aren't going to escape me. Not by a long shot, I'm afraid. So hand over the basket, and step away from the old bag."

Kiki is a braver boy than he has ever thought. "You'll have to fight me first."

"Oh, my dear child." Sir Alistair's laughter seems to rustle the grass round their feet. "You can't be serious."

Betty Friedman puts a hand on their shoulders. "Now," she says, without actually speaking. "Now is the time to run." And she swings them round and shoves them forward, into the ancient circle of stones.

So Near and Yet So Far

Time is indeed a funny thing. One second Kiki and Trish are hurling themselves into the stone circle in the nineteenth century, and the next they are sitting between a Ford Escort and a Toyota Corolla in the car park of The Wat.

"Crikey!" Trish stares up at the dirty tower block that rises into the sky above them with its graffitied walls, sad, flowerless balconies and cracked windows. "That don't look half bad, does it?"

And Kiki, who for so long has dreamed of being back where the tallest thing not a mountain was a tree, says, "I've never been so happy to see anything in my life."

Betty Friedman, however, is unmoved by these tender feelings for home. "Well, that's that sorted." She brushes some dirt from her skirt. "Now we'd better get a move on if we want to get to that meeting before it's too late."

"Too late?" Trish gives a small, nervous laugh. "But, Betty, the meeting was days ago."

"Rubbish. I'm a better Time Keeper than that." Betty Freedman pulls a silver pocket watch from her jacket. "It only started twenty minutes ago. There's still time." She holds out her hand to Trish. "Give me the documents."

Trish hands her the basket.

Betty Friedman lifts the lid to look inside. "Excellent. I see you even kept my shawl. What a nice touch." Satisfied, she slips the basket over her arm. "Now let's—" She breaks off her sentence, dropping silently back between the cars.

"What's wrong?" asks Kiki.

Betty Friedman sighs. "I'm afraid it looks as if Sir Alistair is one step ahead of us. Again."

Trish peeks over the boot of the Ford, half-expecting to see Sir Alistair waving at them from the road. "I don't see nothing."

"Don't you? What about the van parked in front of St Barnabas? And the one over at the entrance to the car park? And the one further along? Not forgetting, of course, the two chaps on either side of the graveyard with the Dobermans."

Kiki risks a peek of his own.

As another example of how funny time can be, not so long ago, when Sir Alistair was trying to reach the Time Portal, the area around The Wat was full of policemen. But now things have returned to normal and, as Betty Friedman pointed out, there are only the vans and security guards and trained-to-maim dogs of the Futures Development Corporation, Ltd.

"Maybe they're just waiting for something…" he suggests.

"Oh that they are…" Betty Friedman's smile is grim. "They're waiting for us."

"It's a good thing we didn't come out in the churchyard," says Trish.

Betty Friedman turns her grim smile on Trish. "I'm not a fool, you know. I always take precautions." Though not always enough, perhaps.

Aggrieved that Betty Friedman isn't showing much gratitude for all they've done, Trish says, "Then how come we didn't land at the Town Hall?"

"I said that I'm not a fool, not that I'm infallible," Betty Friedman retorts. "And you might recall that I had a lot on my mind at the time."

"So now what do we do?" asks Kiki.

Feeling contrite, Trish looks at Betty Friedman. "Have you got a plan?"

"Not precisely," she admits. "They know what we look like, of course – there's no way we can get past them without being spotted."

292

"Maybe we could make ourselves invisible," Kiki suggests.

Betty Friedman shakes her head. "Sadly, though it is certainly a useful skill, it isn't one that I possess."

"I know!" Trish has remembered something else she learned from the telly. "We need to create a distraction. You know, get them to pay attention to something else so we can sneak past them."

"And how do you intend to do that?" Betty Friedman wants to know. "I count seven men, including the two in the churchyard. I don't see how we can get the attention of all of them at once."

"Well, what if we set fire to something?" This ploy has worked any number of times in films Trish has seen.

"Pardon?" Betty Friedman eyes her with a certain amount of concern. "Are you suggesting that we torch one of these automobiles?"

"Well … no…" mumbles Trish, who has been thinking just that. "But there is a lot of rubbish about…"

"Things don't look too good, do they?" Kiki whispers.

Betty Friedman starts to say that things looked considerably better for Napoleon at the start of the Battle of Waterloo but gets no further than

"Napoleon". The explosion of several bangers at the back of Wat Tyler House cuts her off, and, almost immediately, The Wat Boys, hoods up, come tearing round the side of the block riding no-hands on their bikes, whooping with laughter.

Kiki (not completely incorrectly) has always thought of The Wat Boys as the descendants of the Roman Army, storming across Europe, demolishing everything in its way. But not right now. Right now, as he watches them do wheelies across the lustreless clumps of grass that pass for a lawn, they look more like a band of avenging spirits – not friendly spirits, perhaps, but possibly not hostile ones, either – assuming, of course, that you could get them on your side.

"Crikey," mutters Trish. "Just when you think things can't get much worse…"

"Maybe things just got better," says Kiki. "I've got an idea."

Trish gives him a doubtful look. "Really? And what's that? That we all start chanting and make a run for it?"

Kiki Monjate's running days, however, seem to be over. "That we get The Wat Boys to create a distraction."

Trish stares at him in silence for a second. "Excuse me? I think whizzing through time has murdered my hearing or something. Did you just say, 'get *The Wat Boys* to create a distraction'?"

Betty Friedman is also staring at him, but more with thoughtfulness than disbelief. "You know…" she murmurs, "that's not a bad idea at all."

"And how's that work, then?" Trish smirks at Kiki. "Have you got some brilliant charm all of a sudden that will make them do what you want?"

Kiki shrugs. "I reckoned I'd just ask them."

"You?" Trish splutters. "Yeah, right. You're going to *talk* to Brendan Clocker. Don't make me laugh."

"But it has to be Kiki," says Betty Friedman. "You're too easy to spot in that charming frock you're wearing and I'm simply too easy to spot. However, if Kiki takes off his jacket he'll be just another boy among several."

"Right." Kiki takes a very deep breath and looks over to where The Wat Boys are still circling the struggling, shabby clumps of grass. "Here goes nothing."

Kiki and The Wat Boys Speak for the First Time

The Wat Boys would have been less surprised to find the entire Arsenal team in their midst than Kiki Monjate. Indeed, they are so surprised that, in a historic break with tradition, not a single taunt or threat leaves their mouths.

It is Brendan Clocker, as leader and general manager of the gang, who recovers first. "Oi!" says Brendan. "What're you doin' here?"

Kiki uncrosses his fingers and takes a mouthful of air. "We need your help."

The Wat Boys' laughter, though more pleasant than that of Sir Alistair Deuce, is still not the sort to encourage feelings of safety or trust.

"I mean it," says Kiki. "We really need your help."

Brendan Clocker grins. "Who's *we*, gippo? You ain't got no friends."

"Yes, I do." Kiki nods to where Betty Friedman

and Trish are hunkered down between the two cars. "That's them hiding over there."

Brendan has never seen an old lady hiding in a car park before. It makes him curious. "Why're they doin' that?"

"'Cos they're too scared of us to come out," says Aidan.

"They are scared," admits Kiki, "but it's not of you."

"Too right," scoffs Brendan. "If they're mates of yours they're scared of their own shadows."

Having already decided that it might be best not to tell The Wat Boys the complete and unabridged truth, Kiki points out the men and their dogs loitering in the churchyard and the men in the vans. "It's them they're scared of. Them and their boss. There's this meeting up the road – in the Town Hall? – and their boss is trying to stop us getting to it."

"Their boss?" hoots Brendan, and the other boys join in. "Who's he, the bleedin' Godfather or something?"

Kiki nods. "Sort of. He's this really rich, important bloke, but he's a totally major criminal and he's trying to do away with Betty Friedman – and me and Trish – because Betty can prove what a crook he is."

This is, without doubt, the funniest thing The

Wat Boys have seen or heard since they tossed Kiki's trainers onto the bus shelter. They practically choke with laughter. One of them nearly comes off his bike.

"You know what your other problem is – I mean, besides being a chicken, ugly gip?" gasps Chris.

Paul answers for him. "He's madder than a cow, that's what."

"Yeah, right..." says Brendan. "Like a major crim would be after *you*." Brendan Clocker, however, is far more intelligent than he seems. Though his voice is filled with sarcasm and scorn, his eyes are moving back and forth from the block to the church and along the road, assessing the situation as any good soldier would.

"It's true," Kiki insists. "I swear it is. It's a matter of life and death. We really need you. You're the only ones who can help us."

No one has ever needed anything from The Wat Boys before, unless it was for them to go away, but if Kiki was hoping to appeal to their better natures it seems possible that they have none.

Brendan Clocker grins. "And what's in it for us, then? What you going to give us if we give you a hand?"

Kiki, of course, has nothing to give them; he's unlikely to get a new pair of trainers in the foreseeable future and they already get his dinner money. But, in one of those rare moments of complete and unexpected understanding, Kiki realizes that Brendan and his mates are more likely to do things they're told they can't do than things they're actually begged to do.

So, instead of pleading or trying to make some sort of deal, Kiki says, "I should've known you wouldn't be up to it. Not that I blame you," he adds quickly. "I mean, it's not just messing round with someone like me, it's really dangerous, isn't it? It was a stupid idea to ask you. I mean, what could you do? Spray your tags on the vans?" He shifts his weight as though ready to return to Trish and Betty Friedman. "You're no match for these blokes. They're the real deal."

The Wat Boys have by now stopped laughing and are looking at Brendan.

"Hang on a minute." Brendan leans over the handlebars of his bike. "Who said we was afraid of some ponce and his muscle?"

"I didn't mean—"

Brendan interrupts. "Who said we wasn't going to help?"

One for the Home Team

The man in the van at the entrance to the car park
(who is, in fact, the head of security of the Future
Developments Corporation, Ltd) is talking to Sir
Alistair Deuce on his mobile phone (yet again).

"Yeah, I'm absolutely sure," the man is saying,
"there's no sign of them. I've got men posted
inside the church and the old vicarage as well as in
the churchyard and out here, just like you said.
Unless they're invisible they haven't turned up."

"Perhaps we should get a few more men in,"
says Sir Alistair. "I don't think you understand
what this woman is capable of."

The head of security, an experienced former soldier, doesn't laugh because, as someone whose job
it has always been to protect the interests of the
powerful and wealthy, he is never less than serious
and stern, but his mouth twitches slightly. He
believes he understands completely the threat

posed by Betty Friedman. "I thought you said she was ninety. If you ask me, the only thing she's capable of is talking us to death."

Sir Alistair, who planned his point of arrival a bit more carefully than his adversary, is currently hovering at the doorway to the room where the council meeting is being held. He glances at his watch. It will be at least another ten minutes before the sale of St Barnabas comes up for discussion. Ten minutes can be a very long time. "You're not paid for your opinion," he snaps. "And in any event, you don't know the old bag like I do. She may look like some doddery old dear but she's got the heart and mind of a warrior king."

The guard's mouth twitches again. "To be frank, unless she's got the army of a warrior king as well I don't see what the problem is. Look, Sir Alistair, you don't have to keep checking in. If the old lady and the kids turn up, my lads and I can handle it. She won't be giving you any trouble."

One of life's great lessons – one the ancient Greeks never tired of mentioning – is that a person can never really be certain what is going to happen next (*Count no man happy until he is dead* was the way the Greeks put it). This is not a lesson the head of security of the Future Developments Corporation, Ltd, has yet learned – but he is about to learn it now.

No sooner has his conversation ended than several bangers go off – one so close to the van that both he and the dog beside him jump.

He pushes the dog off his lap. "Oh, for God's sake…" says the head of security for the Future Developments Corporation, Ltd. "It's just a bang—"

The rest of his sentence is lost in another flurry of explosions. The head of security opens his door and leans out to see who's throwing the bangers just as a swarm of bicycles circles the van like a party of Sioux surrounding a wagon train. "What do you lot think you're doing?" he roars.

In answer, one of the cyclists whacks the front of the van with a heavy piece of wood, and they all start whooping and yelling as they speed into the car park.

"You bloody yobs!" screams the guard, and he jumps out of the van to give chase.

As soon as he hits the ground, the passenger door opens and a hand reaches in to grab his mobile from the seat and his keys from the ignition. "Oi!" shouts Brendan, holding up these trophies. "Look what I got!"

This brings the man from the van in front of St Barnabas running.

Another barrage of explosions cracks through the afternoon.

"Oi!" shouts Chris from the passenger side of the second van. "Will you look what I found left all on its own? People are so bloody careless." He holds up another mobile and clutch of car keys.

By now the two men in the churchyard, the man in the vicarage, the man in the church and the man in the third van have worked out that something untoward is going on and have joined their comrades.

The security men are far too occupied to notice Betty Friedman, Kiki and Trish slip out from between the Ford Escort and the Toyota Corolla and position themselves expectantly on the kerb.

It is only when Brendan Clocker gives a shrill whistle and the bikes all turn around suddenly and head back out of the car park, three of them stopping briefly to pick up passengers, that the head of security for the Future Developments Corporation, Ltd, realizes he's made a really big mistake.

"Stop those bloody kids!" he bellows, but it is a hollow and completely futile gesture. The security men are all overweight and out of shape and already exhausted from pelting round the car park: there is nothing they can do but watch the bikes disappear up the road.

* * *

"I do want to thank you and your friends for helping us like this." Betty Friedman looks over Brendan Clocker's right shoulder while Mrs Calabash, in full hovering helicopter mode, peers over his left as they race up the hill to the Town Hall.

"'S'all right," says Brendan graciously. Brendan is beginning to appreciate that mischief with a purpose is far more rewarding than mischief without. "We ain't had this much fun ever."

"Well that's good." Betty Friedman sighs. "I shouldn't think that the fun is over yet. We still have to get into that meeting."

"What's the problem?" asks Brendan. "They can't stop you going into a public meeting."

But as the bikes near the Town Hall it becomes apparent that *they* probably can stop Betty Friedman from going into the meeting. They are certainly going to try.

"Cor!" Brendan gives a low whistle. "Look at all the coppers. It's like they're expecting some big demo."

"No, just us."

Brendan glances over his shoulder at her. "Who are you, really?"

"Never mind that now. Go round the back," orders Betty Friedman. "Perhaps we can get in through there."

But Brendan, who has several brave and wily warriors at the top of his family tree, is a natural and aggressive strategist and has inherited the belief that the best defence is a strong offence. "Nah. I've got a better idea."

"You mean straight up the steps?" asks Betty Friedman. "Well, I suppose that will save some time."

He veers left, heading straight for the line of policemen in front of the entrance. Whooping joyously, The Wat Boys follow.

In his excitement and conceptual daring, Brendan has temporarily forgotten about things like doors, but the officers of the law haven't. They step aside to let the bikes jump the few steps to the entrance – where they will be forced to stop rather abruptly.

"Blinkin' heck," Brendan mutters as the closed doors loom in front of them, and, interestingly enough, he does exactly what Kiki on the bike behind him does – which is to shut his eyes.

The Rt Honourable Edward I. Chumbley has finished his spiel about all the benefits the community will receive when the Future Developments Corporation, Ltd, purchases St Barnabas. He smiles out at the few interested citizens and the journalists from the local papers who have bothered to attend, and for the first time since that batty old bag barged into his office feels able to relax and think about the palatial villa he plans to build in a place where the sun always shines and he won't have to pay taxes. Obviously, The Rt Honourable Edward I. Chumbley isn't up on his Greeks either.

For even as he smiles a little more and, with a meaningful look at the councillors, says, "I take it that there aren't any objections to the proposal," the door to the room opens and the guard runs in.

The guard is gibbering. "Through the door … right through the door … right through the door…"

"What the hell are you on about?" demands Mr Chumbley. "Speak up, man!"

Beside him, Sir Alistair leans back in his chair with a sigh, proof that living through the millennia tends to make one philosophical. "He's trying to tell you that they came through a closed door, Edward, that's what he's on about."

"They?" snaps Mr Chumbley. "They who?"

Sir Alistair points to the bikers that have followed the guard into the meeting and are screeching to a halt in front of the committee table. "They *them*."

"See here— I say—" splutters Mr Chumbley.

As you know, Sir Alistair Deuce has not been

overburdened with good qualities, but he does have at least one: he can appreciate intelligence in others. It has been a long time since anyone has outwitted him – a long, long time. The pleasure it gives him to have a worthy opponent at last far outweighs the anger caused by his defeat. Which is why he merely smiles at the old woman sliding off the first bike with her cat. "Ah, my dear… why is it I can never remember your name?" He snaps his fingers. "Oh, yes, now I remember – Betty. My dear, dear Betty. You never change. Remember that time in Parthia? You always have liked to make an entrance, haven't you?"

And Stories Have to End Somewhere

Time has passed, as it does, and in the months of that passing quite a bit has happened.

Unfortunately, not all that has happened has been good. After apologizing to Kiki's parents for the fright Kiki's disappearance gave them, and to Trish's mother for the fright Trish's disappearance would have given her if she hadn't been doing a tour of local pubs and had realized Trish was missing, Betty Friedman herself disappeared. "It's like we dreamt her," said Trish woefully. "She was better than a dream," said Kiki.

But some of what has happened has been very good indeed. Kiki is now very visible to everyone, Trish has stopped feeling responsible for her mother's abyss of unhappiness, and The Wat Boys, unexpectedly (perhaps) given the opportunity to labour on the development of St Barnabas from a ruin to a museum, education centre and national treasure, no longer feel that they have nothing to lose. And St Barnabas was saved. Before she left, Betty Friedman made sure of that. She also made Mr Chumbley, who had no interest in going to jail, promise that not only would local people be employed by the regeneration project, but that a percentage of any monies made by the museum and education centre would be used by the community to encourage small businesses.

It is now a warm summer's evening long after Betty Friedman, Kiki, Trish and The Wat Boys made their memorable entrance at the Council meeting. Not that the event has been forgotten. On the contrary, it is because of that eleventh-hour arrival that St Barnabas – a new plaque by the front door declaring it a World Heritage Site – stands straight and tall against the pink-tinged sky. The church's brickwork has been repaired and cleaned, and its doors and windows replaced. Its immaculate lawn is planted with wild flowers. Even the clock in the bell tower, whose hands hadn't moved in nearly a hundred and fifty years, is working again. Tomorrow St Barnabas will be opened to the general public, with a reception for local residents in the site's offices in the restored vicarage, but today is the official opening. A wide, deep blue ribbon stretches across the main entrance, and in front of this ribbon we find Mr Edward I. Chumbley, the new Minister for Culture. Mr Chumbley is giving a speech.

A sizeable group of people the government considers important stands at the foot of the church steps, listening patiently to Mr Chumbley's speech. This group is made up of archaeologists, scholars, historians, artists, public servants, celebrities, politicians, a famous rock musician and a less-famous representative from the United Nations.

Behind this group – closer to the pavement than the church – stands a much smaller group of people the government doesn't consider all that important. This group is made up of Kiki Monjate, Trish O'Leary and The Wat Boys – all of whom have been invited to tomorrow's ceremony with their families but who somehow felt obliged to witness this one too. As Brendan Clocker put it, "It's our church, ain't it? The old lady'd expect us to be here."

Mr Chumbley finally finishes banging on about all the work, money and vision that have made this day possible – the careful restoration, the even more careful excavation, the belief that there are things more important than luxury flats – and prepares to present the representative from the United Nations to cut the ribbon. "And now," he says, "it gives me great pleasure to introduce to you some

310

people whose help and support has been invaluable to this project." He pauses, smiling, and then opens his mouth and, to his and everyone else's surprise, says, "Miss Trisha O'Leary and Mr Kiki Monjate."

Miss Trisha O'Leary and Mr Kiki Monjate look at each other.

"Go on!" Brendan Clocker jabs Kiki in the ribs. "That's you!"

Neither Kiki nor Trish makes a move.

"You heard Brendan," says a voice behind them. A hand pushes firmly on each of their backs. "Get up there. This is your success, not Mr Chumbley's."

Trish, Kiki and The Wat Boys all turn round.

It is Betty Friedman in her patchwork skirt and combat boots, her carpetbag slung over one shoulder and Mrs Calabash sound asleep over one arm.

"Oi, Miss Friedman!" cry The Wat Boys, clearly happy to see her. "Where've you been?"

Kiki is too pleased to say anything.

"Betty!" Trish throws herself at Betty Friedman and wraps her arms around her. "You came back! I knew you would! I knew you'd come back!"

"Well, of course I came back," snaps Betty Friedman. "I wouldn't miss this, would I?"

"But how?" asks Kiki. "We thought you were gone for good."

"Don't be ridiculous. I'm never gone for good."
Betty Friedman disentangles herself from Trish
and gives them both a gentle shove. "We'll have
plenty of time to catch up later," she says, "but
now you and go cut that silly ribbon. Think how
thrilled your parents will be to see you on the
evening news."

This is what the thousands (possibly millions) of
people who will come to St Barnabas to be
reunited with the past will find. The body of the
church is now a museum that chronicles the history of the site from pagan times to the present
day, exhibiting some of the important artefacts
that have been discovered – from bronze daggers
and Roman coins to golden goblets and a broken
sandal. In one corner, flanked by old photographs
and newspaper articles, the visitor may sit on a
pew where the bums of several people who wrote
some very good poems once sat, and listen
through headphones to the voices of long-lived
locals talk about their lives and all the changes
they have seen. Or they may go down to the two
levels below where quite a few people who once
walked above ground now reside. One section of
the floor of the medieval crypt is made of glass,
allowing the visitor to see the sacred burial ground
beneath it. The sword of the great Celtic king is on

display upstairs, but his remains – once deeply buried in a corner of the churchyard – have been moved to lie beneath the church, marked by the carefully illuminated, precious Ogham stone.

The important guests have gone to the reception in the vicarage and The Wat Boys have gone home, but it is here, looking down on the stone, that Betty Friedman, Kiki and Trish resume the conversation begun outside St Barnabas, while Mrs Calabash, curled up between the children, purrs gently in her sleep.

Betty Friedman had the foresight to bring a flask of tea and a tin of biscuits with her, and now she pours tea into the three cups she also had the foresight to bring.

"This is nice, isn't it?" says Betty Friedman as she hands them their cups. "The three of us enjoying a nice cup of tea together again."

"Just like when we first met you." Kiki helps himself to a biscuit. "Except that we weren't in a crypt then."

"And except that me and Kiki weren't heroes then, either," says Trish.

"I don't know about being heroes, but you certainly did a very difficult job – and did it well." Betty Freedman sips her tea. "We'd be sitting in a car park now if it weren't for you two."

The mention of car parks reminds Kiki of someone who might have been expected to be amongst the dignitaries at the ceremony. "What happened to Sir Alistair? I sort of thought he'd be hanging out with Mr Chumbley and that lot today."

Betty Friedman rests her cup on her knee. "I appreciate how sorry you'll be to hear this – and I do so hate to be the bearer of bad news – but I'm afraid that Sir Alistair Deuce is no longer with us."

"Is that why you vanished like that?" asks Trish. "'Cos you went off to kill him?"

"You really do have a penchant for drama, don't you, Trish?" Betty Friedman hands her a serviette. "Of course I didn't kill him. Which isn't to say that I haven't been tempted once or twice … in Albion, for example, and that time in Alexandria. But I do not believe in violence. No, no, Sir Alistair has moved on to destroy something else."

"So where were you?" Trish demands. "Did you go back to save Constance?"

"Oh, dear Constance. No, that's not why I left." Betty Friedman smiles sadly. "I'm afraid I can't save Constance, Trish, as I should think you'd understand. My job is one of damage control more than anything else. I told you before, I can't go back in time and make things different."

"But why not?" Trish persists. "She helped us."

"Yes, I know she did. But, for one thing, if I freed her everything that touched her life would be changed. And what would happen to me?"

"You mean because she was you?" asks Kiki.

"I think it would be more accurate to say that I was she, Kiki. But whichever way you put it, it would upset the sequence of my lives – as well as upsetting everything I've done and affected as Betty Friedman, which, I assure you, is quite a bit. So I'm afraid that Constance will have to live out what time is left to her in Dr Prole's asylum."

"Is it going to be a long time?" asks Kiki.

Betty Friedman shakes her head. "No, dear, I shouldn't think it will be too long. Time Keepers can't afford to languish. There's too much to be done."

Trish looks at Betty Friedman. "You know what else I don't get?"

"No, dear Trish, what don't you get?"

"Well, Dr Prole said he was going to rebuild the church – you know, so he could get at the treasure and all – but he didn't. It was all still here. He left it alone."

"Not by choice, I assure you." Betty Friedman takes another sip of tea. "I believe that if you look up the newspapers of the time, you'll see that Dr Prole had a very unfortunate accident that put an end to both his plans for the church and his greed once and for all."

"Really?" says Trish. "You mean like he was run over or something?"

"I mean like a very large piece of masonry fell on him while he was searching for the Time Portal." Betty Friedman hides the very slightest of smiles behind her teacup. "What one might call being hoisted by his own petard."

Kiki, who has been staring through the glass floor, looks up. "What's that mean?"

"Own goal," says Trish.

Kiki nods, but he turns his eyes back to the Ogham stone, looking as if there is something else that he doesn't get.

Betty Friedman touches his shoulder. "What is it?"

"Nothing." Kiki shrugs. "It's just that it seems sort of sad that nobody really knows what the stone says." The stone is so worn and the carving such a primitive form of Ogham that the experts could make no more than a general and incomplete guess.

"Don't they?" Betty Friedman gazes up at the ceiling rather than down at the grave and recites from memory, "'So long as there is one voice, truth cannot be silenced. So long as there is one heart, what is loved can never die.'"

"That's a funny thing to say about a king," suggests Trish.

316

"Not this king," says Betty Friedman. "It says what's important."

Kiki frowns. "What about that last bit? Is that last bit about the woman with the red hair – you know, the one who cries by the stone?"

"Ah, *that* woman." Betty Friedman sighs. She should have known he'd seen the woman. "What makes you think it has something to do with her?"

He shrugs again. "It said in the paper that the king's skeleton had a bracelet made of red hair round one wrist and she has red hair. And she has a bracelet like that, only the hair is dark. So, you know, I thought that maybe they loved each other."

"I think you're taking it too literally." Betty Friedman starts gathering up the cups. "That woman wasn't the only one who loved him. He was very special – not only a great and wise leader of men, but of souls as well. He was – is – loved by the universe itself."

Trish watches Betty Friedman whisk the cups and biscuit tin into her carpetbag. "Are we going or something?"

"I'm afraid so. I really must be getting on."

"Getting on where?" asks Kiki. "You only just got here."

"This was just a brief visit. I thought you understood that."

"I didn't," says Trish. "I thought you were going to stay for a while."

"There's no way I can do that. I made a special trip to be here for the official opening of St Barnabas." Seeing their disappointed faces, she suddenly leans forward and puts an arm around each of them. "And to see you, of course. You're the best helpers I've ever had."

Kiki straightens up from her embrace, rubbing what may be a speck of dust from his eye.

"I've got an idea, Betty," says Trish. "Why don't I go with you wherever it is you're off to? Now that I know how things work – and you know how helpful I am. I could give you a hand. You're not getting any younger, you know."

Betty Friedman stands up, slipping the carpet-bag over her shoulder. "That's very kind of you, dear, but I need you here." She holds out her hands and pulls them both to their feet. "The two of you. To keep an eye on things. We can never relax our guard, you know."

"But we don't have any power," says Kiki.

"How many times do I have to tell you? You both have power – very special power – all the power you need."

"Only I'll miss you," Trish mumbles.

Betty Friedman squeezes her hand. "And I'll miss you." She squeezes Kiki's hand. "And you.

wisdom, Trish hurries past him. "I'm going home," she states. "I don't want to talk no more."

"Trish!" Kiki grabs at the leg of her jeans. "Trish, don't you want to know what I think?"

"No," says Trish, trying to pull away. "I blinkin' well don't."

"I think Betty Friedman left this behind. For you. You know, like a sign."

And he hands her the blue glove that was lying by the gate.

And so will Mrs Calabash." Mrs Calabash, draped over her owner's arm, opens her golden eyes and purrs. "But you must remember that this is a strange and wondrous world – you never can tell when we might meet again."

Trish isn't interested in possibilities, only certainties. "Does that mean we *will* meet again? You know, like, for sure you'll come back for us when you need our help?"

There is no answer. And there is no answer because they aren't in the crypt with Betty Friedman and Mrs Calabash any more, but on the steps of St Barnabas by themselves.

The lights of the vicarage shine in the darkening night and laughter rolls through its walls. The severed blue ribbon flutters in the breeze.

"So that's it." Trish snuffles back her tears as they walk down the steps. "Hello. Goodbye. Just like that. Like we really don't matter at all."

"You don't know," comforts Kiki. "She said she's never really gone, didn't she? She said we might meet her again."

"That's as good as saying we might not," mumbles Trish.

Kiki, however, has spotted something on the ground and is bending down to pick it up. "Trish?"

Thinking he is about to offer her more words of